The Exception

The Exception

BRITTANY WYNNE

This book is a work of fiction. Any references to historical events, real people, or real places are used fictitiously. Other names, characters, places, and events are products of the author's imagination, and any resemblance to actual events or places or persons, living or dead is entirely coincidental.

Copyright © 2015 Brittany Wynne

Cover Design: Sarah Hansen, Okay Creations

ISBN 978-0-692-42727-9

For my husband Chris,

The boy who swept me off my feet.

Jake

After I got hurt, coach didn't make me attend practice. He told me to let myself heal and then worry about the physical therapy side of things. And that is exactly what I did. I spent my entire junior year letting my arm recover and then working with a personal trainer.

Hell, since that night I have hardly looked at a drink – much less had one. I never thought one fight could get so out of hand. I worked so hard for that top singles seed. Now I'd be playing boy's doubles, at best. Fan-freaking-tastic.

The first day of practice my senior year, I had the right mind to walk straight up to coach and tell him I was done. I didn't need another P.E. credit, and after a year of being out, I was sure my spot had long been filled. But then I saw her. She was on one of the top courts, surrounded by a few guys from the team and some other girl I didn't know.

I wasn't sure about a lot of things going into this year, but in that moment I knew I needed to be near her. I needed to kiss those lips and breathe her in. A girl like that, I bet she smelled damn good.

I was about to walk right up to her and snatch her away before any of those other pricks had a chance, but one simple move stopped me dead in my tracks. One of the guys snaked his arm around her waist, letting his fingers drag across the small of her back, and then whispered something in her ear. Whatever he said made her laugh, and I found myself clenching my fists at my side. I didn't even know this chick, and yet she was already getting a reaction out of me.

I took a deep breath as I stretched my fingers out. This was crazy. I haven't felt the urge to take a swing at someone since that night and still, then I'd had a few. I was completely sober, but all that long, blonde hair made me want to assault that guy, who was probably her boyfriend.

I shook my head as I took a step back. I hadn't been that guy for about a year now, and I wasn't about to go back. I have worked too hard to get where I am. Even if she is the most beautiful girl I have ever seen. Even when just looking at her fills me with some primal instinct to make her mine. She was taken, and I was going to respect that. A girl like that deserves respect. And this is the new Jake Reynolds, damn it!

Chapter One

"How long have they been playing?" I asked as I positioned myself on the bleachers next to my best friend, simultaneously taking off my hat and trying to salvage my ponytail.

"Just started the third set," Maya quickly answered, before turning back to shamelessly flirt with Dylan.

It was near the end of a long Friday, as I watched Ryan bounce that little neon green ball several times before tossing it up to serve. I was still amazed that I managed to successfully complete all my matches. Just this morning, my mom was running me to the small town pharmacy to try and find something to settle my stomach. Deciding on an old-fashioned remedy suggested by the pharmacist, my mother insisted that I sip the concoction as she drove back to the courts. It was not easy to choke down a thick, sweet, coke-flavored syrup when you're already queasy, but my mom was desperate because it was the first tennis tournament of the season. She would have tried anything that would possibly allow me to play.

Through the nausea, I smiled when my mom wished me a happy seventeenth birthday before giving me the estimated time before my second match. My mother had always been the competitive type. See, though every coach that I ever had told me I had natural ability and was lucky to be tall and left handed, I didn't have a competitive bone in my body. I like to believe that it was because my mother had all of them and there was none left for me when I came along. I had better be on my deathbed before I missed out on a tennis tournament.

"Right, Emma?" Maya said, shoving an elbow in my side.

"Huh, what?" I managed when I realized I had missed out on the conversation.

"You haven't listened to a single word I said," Maya pouted with a forced frown. Beaming, she continued, "I was just telling the boys the plan for your birthday party tomorrow night."

"Sounds like the same back to school bash as always." Dylan joined in, leaning forward around Maya, winking at me with his best Dylan Andrews smile.

"Y'all are obviously up to something, but I'm too pooped to make you spill!" I joked, reaching across Maya to shove Dylan's arm.

I was an August baby, and my birthday always fell sometime during the first week of school. Therefore, my birthday party was always the first Friday after school started. Every year it signaled the giant pool party in my parents' over-sized backyard. This year my birthday was on a Friday, but so was the first tennis tournament of the year. So the birthday party was pushed back to Saturday.

"Hey, who's that guy playing with Ryan?" I asked, just noticing the tall guy with tousled dark brown hair whose smile made me want to be near him. "Is he new?"

I watched as he skillfully darted to the other side of the net and ended the point with ease, unable to tear my eyes away from how his calf and arm muscles flexed in the process.

Maya looked at me with her famous "you're an idiot" smirk before replying, "That's Jake Reynolds. He's a senior. And, no, he is not new."

Dylan leaned back to slap Gabe, who was on the row directly behind us, and mocked, "Is he new," and all three burst into laughter. "My God, Em. Have you been living under a rock?"

I blushed while pulling a loose piece of hair that had fallen from my ponytail behind my ear. "Whatever." I rolled my eyes while giving my best attempt to act annoyed.

"Nice shot, Ryan!" I yelled, looking up just in time to see Ryan end a point. The two high-fived, and I couldn't help but notice the way Jake ran his fingers through his hair afterwards – or how it made me want to do the same thing. *Jeez Emma, get a grip. You don't need to be fantasizing about running your fingers through some random guy's hair. Even if it does hang perfectly right above his eyes.* I couldn't keep from wondering what color his eyes were.

5

But framed with all that dark hair, I bet any color would pop. *Good grief. You need to pull it together.*

Maya looked at me like she was going to say something but changed her mind and returned her attention to Dylan. When it was obvious that Maya was distracted Gabe leaned forward, still munching on his trail mix, and whispered, "Like what you see?" with a nervous grin.

It was no secret that Gabe liked me, and though he tried to play it cool I could see it bothered him when he caught me starring at Jake.

"Oh shut up." I said smiling, then leaned back against Gabe. He instinctually wrapped his arms around me and replied, "Just looking after my best gal pal."

"I don't need looking after. Besides, I'm just trying to figure out, if he's not new, how we played on the same team for a year and I never noticed him before." I reached back and playfully pinched Gabe's side.

"Hey, hey, hey, OK!" Gabe laughed, throwing his hands in the air signaling his surrender and then wrapping his arms back around me and squeezing me tight. "I'm just waiting for you to look at me the way you looked at some guy you don't even know," he whispered.

I closed my eyes and breathed in. It's not that I didn't like Gabe; it's just that I didn't want to ruin our friendship by starting something that may not work. I mean, sure he is handsome with his deep brown eyes and rugged good looks, but we just were missing that chemistry or spark that an actual relationship needs, at least on my end. I heard him let out a defeated sigh as he breathed out, and I knew he wouldn't mention it again. So I settled back into his arms, and we watched the rest of the match.

We all stood and cheered as Ryan and Jake shook their opponents' hands at the net at the end of their match. Ryan was beaming when he turned to face us, knowing he and Jake were taking home first place in boy's doubles and securing the overall win for our team. When the four of us rushed to the gate to congratulate Ryan, I found myself looking for Jake. During all the excitement, he somehow had disappeared. Before I could give it another thought, Dylan threw his arms around my and Maya's shoulders shouting, "First victory of the year! Let's celebrate!"

Laughing, I shrugged off Dylan's arm. "It's gunna be a long year," I teased.

"You turn that frown upside down birthday girl." Dylan shot back, obviously unfazed. He wrapped his arms around a squealing Maya as the five of us made it back to my mom's car.

One of the things I loved about small tournaments, at the start of the season, is that we didn't have to ride the school bus. There was something fun about just the five of us in my mom's SUV. Plus, she always stopped for donuts before we left town.

At my mom's car, Dylan pulled back the seat so Ryan and Gabe could climb into the back row. Once he closed the seat, he jumped in and slid across, patting the spot next to him while looking at Maya. Why those two didn't just admit their feelings for each other is beyond me.

7

I shook my head as I climbed in, and Ryan gave me a knowing glance.

The entire drive home I couldn't stop thinking about Jake, and I found myself looking forward to Monday when I could see him again. I realized I was smiling when Maya gawked, "Oh no, I've seen that look before." I shot her a look and she responded "alright" pretending to lock her mouth with a key and tossing it to the back seat at Ryan who pretended to dodge it. "But only because it's your birthday!" she exclaimed, hugging me. "Now let's talk about what we are going to wear tomorrow."

"Do you two have to do this right now?" Maya turned to the right to look at Dylan who had a sly smile spreading across his face. "Well, then how do you expect me to plan my outfit if you two are planning yours?"

"Andrews, do you ever stop talking?" Ryan chimed in. "I'm beginning to think you just like the sound of your own voice." He continued while leaning forward to deck Dylan in the arm.

Dylan swooped his hair to the side, casting those bright green eyes in our direction; he gave us a smoldering look. "I'm Dylan Andrews. Everyone likes the sound of my voice," he replied with his best Chuck Bass impression.

"You have been watching way too much Gossip Girl on Netflix!" I giggled.

"I happen to like that show." He said coolly, adjusting his shirt.

8

"And here I thought it was all part of your try to date Maya plan." Ryan added, dramatically covering his mouth. "Oops!"

I could feel Maya's excitement as she squeezed my hand while Dylan responded, "Ryan, you're such a douche." Then he turned his attention to Gabe on the other side of the backseat "You've been very quiet back there, Gabriel."

"Just tired. Some of us actually played tennis today." Gabe said coldly.

"Jeez. Don't get your panties in a wad." Dylan replied, pretending to be offended. Maya and Ryan looked up at him. He gave a confused shrug, playing up his hurt feelings act – cueing Maya to scoot closer.

"Did he hurt your wittle feelings?" She teased in a baby voice.

He nodded while tilting his head down and puckering his bottom lip. He began to pull her closer when my mom jumped in, "Dylan, not in my backseat. Save your smooth moves for another time and place." she said, cracking herself up.

Embarrassed, the two quickly separated and Dylan responded, "You got it Mrs. C. Anything for my favorite mom."

I rolled my eyes. "Dylan you're such a suck up."

"Now Emma, don't be rude to my favorite adopted son," she chuckled.

"You're just as bad as he is!" I said, no longer able to contain my laughter.

I had forgotten Gabe's bad mood until he was the only one I didn't hear laughing. Turning to the backseat, I saw him gazing out the window into the dark and my laughter stopped. Luckily, the other three were still joking with my mom and didn't notice the absence of Gabe and I in the conversation.

"Gabe," I said softly as to not alert the others, "what's up with you?" I knew my recent discovery of Jake's existence had something to do with it. At the sound of my voice directed at him, his mood seemed to lighten.

"So now you want to talk to me," he whispered. Seeing my confused expression he continued, "Don't look at me like that. You haven't said one word to me since we left the bleachers," he finished, reaching up to tuck a piece of hair behind my ear.

"Oh." I pursed my lips together, realizing his mood wasn't just about Jake but also because my attention had previously been completely occupied. I probably shouldn't mention that it was Jake that had me so distracted.

"Don't do that, Em. Don't lose your smile because of me."

"I didn't..." I began.

"Hey," he interrupted me. "Don't apologize because I don't like you being interested in another guy."

OK. So maybe he did know that it was Jake that had me so distracted.

"I'm the one that should be apologizing. Now, let's move past this and talk about more important things," he said with that impossible, boyish smile of his starting to

10

make its way onto his face. "What do you want for your birthday?"

Gabe always could make me feel better. Somehow he always said and did the right thing to make me smile. He truly was my best guy friend. So after watching that smile creep across his face I promptly countered, pointing my finger in his direction and looking as stern as I could without laughing, "One, I am not interested in Jake. I don't even know him. And two, you know you don't have to get me anything for my birthday." Completely giving into the smile that I had been fighting back, I added, "Although if you were to get me something..." Before I could finish Gabe was leaning over the seat pulling me back with him, which made me erupt into giggles as I pretended to fight him off.

"Em! Watch it!" Maya shouted as I was being pulled over the backseat.

"I'll save you!" Dylan proclaimed, taking advantage of the moment to put his arm back around Maya.

Ryan started laughing at the whole ordeal and shook his head, "Why do I even put up with you people?"

"Hey, hey, hey. Cool it you two. I can't worry about you, drive this car, and keep my eye on Mr. Romance over there at the same time," my mother stated flatly.

"Cooling it," Gabe replied as he settled me onto his lap, looking me in the eyes as he spoke.

"Mom, you have nothing to worry about. You know Gabe and I are just friends," I said while playfully squeezing one of his cheeks. I wasn't sure if I had said that out loud more to reassure my mother or Gabe.

11

"Best friends," he countered touching his forehead to mine, keeping his arms wrapped tightly around my waist.

"Best friends," I whispered back.

The rest of the ride home I listened to my friends plan my birthday. OK, Maya planned my birthday, but to be fair the guys did have some ideas – like sneaking in a keg – cueing my mother to threaten their lives and cancel the whole thing. She probably would have been more intimidating if she didn't think the guys were kidding. Each time the guys suggested something else Maya was quick to dismiss their "silly" comments with her hand while she kept planning, never missing a beat. By the time we got to Ryan's house I knew what time the party started, the theme, the playlist for the night, and who was on the invite list. I had to admit that Maya could plan a fun party, and I was pretty excited. We dropped the other two boys off, then headed back to my house.

Maya was staying for the weekend because her parents were out of town, which worked out great since it was my birthday weekend. By the time we got home we were both exhausted, so we said goodnight to my parents and went upstairs to my room. Just as we were climbing into bed, there was a knock at my window.

"I'm going to kill him."

"How is he not asleep? I'm so tired!" Maya whined.

"Maybe he'll think we're asleep," I yawned as I pulled the covers up to my neck.

Not two seconds later, my window was being lifted up and Gabe was climbing through, not bothering to stop on his way to my bathroom as Maya and I complained about how late it was.

"Be right back," I uttered groggily, throwing the covers back and getting out of bed.

"Mhmm. Night, Em." Maya muttered as she dozed off.

I walked into my bathroom, and Gabe was sitting in the bowl chair. Once he saw me, he motioned for me to come sit with him. My bathroom was pretty big, so we actually hung out in there a lot. The guys always joked that we needed to put a TV in there.

Once I was standing in front of him, he pulled me down onto his lap. "I know it's late, but I wanted to give you this while it was still your actual birthday." He put a small wrapped present in my hand and waited for me to open it.

I couldn't help but smile. Gabe was always doing thoughtful things like this for me. I unwrapped the present to reveal a black velvet box. I knew it was some kind of jewelry, but when I opened the lid I gasped. It was the white gold bracelet with the butterfly charm that I had been wanting. "Oh, Gabe, it's perfect!" I gushed. "How'd you know?"

"I saw the way you looked at it every time we went to the mall and you and Maya drug us to the jewelry store," he said sheepishly. "So, do you like it?"

"Like it? I love it! Thank you so much, Gabe!" I threw my arms around him to give him a hug and kiss on the cheek. "Here, help me put it on!" I squealed, holding out my wrist so Gabe could hook the clasp.

"You are more than welcome," he said with a huge smile on his face. "But it's officially after midnight and you have a big day tomorrow with what Maya has planned, so I guess I better be going." We both stood up and I followed behind him as he walked across my room to my window, both of us being quiet so we didn't wake up Maya.

"Thanks again, Gabe," I smiled unable to tear my eyes away from my new bracelet.

"Anything for you, Em." I heard him utter under his breath while climbing out my window. "Night, Em, see you later today," he said with a wink and in a voice meant for me to hear this time.

"Night, Gabe."

Chapter Two

"Emma! Wake up!" I heard before a pillow made contact with my face.

"Five more minutes." I groaned.

"Em!" Smack. There was the pillow again.

"Alright, I'm up." I said groggily, willing myself to move before I was attacked by another pillow.

"Good. It's about time. I've been trying to wake you up for the past five minutes because we have a ton to do today. We have to go get your new license, get our nails done, go to the mall to get new bikinis, and still be back here in time to get set up and dressed for the party," Maya exclaimed.

She may be my best friend, but that girl was entirely too perky in the morning. I've always been more of a sleep-till-noon type person unless I had to get up for school. Maya, on the other hand, thought nine o'clock was sleeping in.

"So the boys are texting everyone the details about today and will be here about four to help set up. Speaking of boys, what time did Gabe leave last night?" she asked with a smirk.

"He was only here for about ten minutes. He just wanted to give me my birthday present on my real birthday," I said. Smiling as I remembered my new bracelet I was wearing, I held my arm out for Maya to see.

"Holy crap, Em. That boy is in love with you."

"He's not in love with me. He's just my best guy friend, and you know he has always been super sweet and thoughtful." I knew Gabe liked me – but loved me? That couldn't be true; that would just make things so weird between us. I mean I loved Gabe, but I was not in love with Gabe and I certainly didn't want to ruin our friendship.

"Whatever, Em, whatever you say," Maya said, dragging out the second whatever.

"Oh shut up," I said sarcastically, throwing my pillow at her.

Within the next thirty minutes, we were both out of bed, had thrown on some clothes and a touch of makeup, and were putting the finishing touches on each of our messy buns. That was record time for the two of us to be up and ready. Then again, we weren't really getting ready yet. We just had to look presentable enough to get our nails done and go to the mall. Plus, I wasn't that worried about my license picture. No one ever sees those things anyway. That's when it hit me for the first time that day. Yes, Maya mentioned it when we were still in bed but I was still trying to wake up then.

"Oh my gosh. I'm seventeen now. I get my Jeep back! Maya, you don't have to drive us everywhere anymore!"

"I was wondering when you were going to show a little excitement about that."

We were both squealing when my mom walked in, giving us a strange look. So I ran to my purse, grabbed the keys that had been in there for a year now, and held them up. Realization hit my mom's face, and for a second I thought she was going to cry before she pulled me into a hug, "Oh, honey, I'm so excited for you! My little girl can drive again." Next thing I knew we were all squealing when my dad popped his head in my room to let us know pancakes were ready. When he saw what was going on he quickly retreated, shaking his head and laughing.

It felt like this day was never going to get here. One little wreck the week I turned sixteen and my license was revoked until my next birthday. No one even got hurt, unless you count the other car's bumper and the front of my car. Apparently, they take it very seriously when you get in a wreck your first year of driving, especially when it is your fault because you were texting. Details.

* * *

We had just sat down in the pedicure chairs when my phone beeped. It was Gabe asking if we needed the boys

17

to grab anything else for the party tonight. I texted back that we were good, but if I thought of anything I'd let him know.

"Wow, that was weird," I murmured.

"What's weird?"

I looked over at Maya in the chair next to me. "Gabe just called me Emmie."

"What?" Maya giggled as I showed her the text I had just gotten from Gabe.

K. C U later Emmie!

Maya shook her head. "Yup, he's got it bad."

Not wanting to start talking about that again, I changed the subject. "So what's up with you and Dylan?"

"Oh, Em, I can't figure that boy out. One minute he's hooking up with anything that moves, and the next he seems like he's into me."

"Well, it's not like you wanted to be more than friends until this summer. Maybe he just doesn't know that the infamous Maya is ready to settle down."

She let out a sigh. "Yeah, but I don't know how I could make it any more obvious that I don't just want to be friends anymore."

I burst out laughing. "Maya, the girl who could have any guy she wanted, suddenly doesn't know how to let a guy know she's into him?"

I could see she was thinking about what I just said, and then she started laughing too.

18

"Well then, I guess I'm going to have to find one hell of a bikini today," she said winking.

"And she's back," I said causing us to laugh even harder.

"Ah, right on time," Maya managed as we were both still laughing.

I turned to see she was looking at Ryan walking in with two large cups in his hand followed by Dylan and Gabe, each carrying a drink of their own.

"Your drinks, ladies," Ryan reached out, handing us each a cup from our favorite place.

"You guys are the best," I said excitedly, taking a drink.

"Just following orders for the birthday girl," Ryan explained, nudging Maya.

"Good little minion," Maya cooed.

I seriously had the best friends in the world. My birthday was technically yesterday, yet here they were making this day as special as they could for me.

"So what's on the agenda next?" Ryan asked.

"Shopping for teenie bikinis," Maya informed as Dylan started choking on his drink.

Gabe chimed in, "Translation, can we come?" causing Dylan's cheeks to turn a shade of pink.

"Why Dylan, is that a blush I see?" I said jokingly.

"More like a I can't breathe after ice went down the wrong pipe," he countered.

"Yeah, yeah," Gabe replied.

"Alright ladies, we have to head out. I promised my mom I'd mow the lawn and take care of some other yard work before the party, and these guys said they'd help." Ryan nodded for the guys to head to the door, then walked that way himself. Dylan gave a quick wave then followed after him.

"See ya in a few hours, Em," Gabe gave me a hug and then told Maya bye as he headed for the door as well.

"Don't you mean Emmie?" Maya called out.

Gabe stopped briefly and then kept walking without turning around.

"Wow. Really?" I looked at Maya as Gabe walked out the front door. She gave a little shrug before taking a big gulp of her drink. I rolled my eyes and then faced forward to check the progress of my toes.

* * *

I had just come out of the dressing room to show Maya the purple two-piece I had tried on when I saw him. Just the sight of him caused my heart to speed up. But he was with some tall, skinny blonde looking at purses in the section across from where we were. *Of course he has a girlfriend. Why wouldn't Mr. tall, dark, and handsome have a girlfriend?*

"Oh that one is cute, Emmie." Maya teased before noticing my face. Realizing I was in somewhat of a trance, she looked the direction I was facing and then a knowing smile crossed her face. "Like what ya see, Em?" she asked.

20

"Huh? What? I was just…"

"You were just drooling over Jake Reynolds again," she giggled. And before I realized what she was doing, she was walking in his direction not caring that she was still wearing the tiny, red, string bikini she had tried on.

Maya had always been confident like that, not that she didn't have a reason not to be. She was a few inches shorter than me, with long brunette hair, honey-colored eyes, olive skin, and a perky C cup that always got her attention from the guys; she was curvy in all the right places. I had more of a boyish figure. Not that I was lacking or anything with my long, blonde hair, blue eyes, and skin that was currently a light tan because it was the end of summer, but my B cups were not her almost D's by any means.

I just stood there as she made her way over to Jake, praying she didn't say anything too embarrassing. I watched as she walked up and turned on her Maya charm, not acknowledging the girl he was with, who looked slightly annoyed, at all. She giggled at something before putting her hand on her hip and pointing in my direction. I immediately pretended like I had no idea she was over there and that I was checking out my swimsuit in the mirror, when they looked my way. I watched the rest of the time through the reflection of the mirror until I saw Maya walking back my direction.

"You could have given me a little heads up that you were going to point at me so I wasn't standing there

21

awkwardly when you all turned to look at me," I said obviously annoyed as I walked back into my dressing room.

"If you're going to act all pissy I guess I won't tell you what we were talking about," she said, following behind me.

"OK." I plopped down in the seat of my dressing room suddenly more excited than I should have been. By the growing smile that was on my face, she knew all was forgiven.

"I told him it was your birthday and that we were having a party at your house and that he should come and bring a swimsuit," she said mischievously.

"What, what is that face?" I asked, knowing all too well that she wasn't telling me something.

"I may have said the party was by invitation only so he couldn't bring a date," she replied as if it were nothing at all.

My jaw dropped. How she had the nerve to say half the stuff she did I will never know. I would have been way too embarrassed to walk up to him, much less half naked, and say something like that, especially in front of some girl who was probably his girlfriend. My mouth was still hanging open from shock when she walked back into her dressing room throwing over a skimpy, black bikini that matched the red one she was wearing. "Try that one on, Em. It's your birthday. You want to look sexy, not cute."

Nope. No way. Me, wearing the black version of what she had on – not going to happen.

"Especially if sex-on-a-stick is going to be there," she added.

OK. It might happen. And did she really just call him that?

When I walked out in her bikini of choice, she smiled and clapped her hands together. "Yep, that's the one! Take it off. I'm buying it for you for your birthday," she exclaimed. I just rolled my eyes and walked back into my dressing room.

"Thanks, slut." I said as I threw the suit over the door to Maya.

"You're welcome, biatch!"

* * *

By the time we made it back to my house, we only had about thirty minutes to get dressed before the boys got there. So I hopped in my shower and Maya went to my sister's room to shower. Once I was out I put on my new black bikini, dried my hair, and had just finished putting on my makeup when my bedroom door opened.

"Turn on some music before you come back here, OK, Maya?"

"It's me." Gabe said walking into my bathroom.

"Gabe, I could have been naked! Knock next time!" I said pretending to scold him.

"Could have been?" Gabe said with a mixture of shock and excitement on his face.

"Ya like?" I asked as I did a little twirl.

"Of course I like it, but so will every guy at the party. Are you really wearing that?" he gawked.

23

"She absolutely is," Maya stated as she walked in, sporting a navy and white-striped cover up. "That's why I bought it for her to wear at her party. So she'd look hot," she said as she smacked me on the butt.

Gabe almost looked like he was in pain. "Em, are you trying to kill me?"

"Nah, we just had to make sure she was on her A game since I invited Jake."

Gabe glared at Maya. "And when did Jake get invited?" Gabe said through his teeth.

"When we ran into him at the mall and I invited him. Sheesh. What's got your panties in a wad?"

"Nothing, considering I don't wear panties," Gabe said harshly.

"OK you two. I'm about to put y'all in time out. Maya, why don't you go see what they have left to do to get ready for the party."

"Okie dokie, boss. She does look hot though, doesn't she, Gabe?" she said, winking at me on the way out of my bathroom.

Gabe sighed as he sank into my bowl chair. "I'm sorry, Em. I didn't mean to upset you on your birthday."

I walked over to him and sank down on his lap, which caused him to suck in a breath. I guess my bikini had more of an effect than I thought. "You didn't upset me, but I'm also not the person you should be apologizing to. What got into you, Gabe?"

"Nothing. I don't know. I mean. You. This," he said, gesturing at my bikini.

24

"Gabe, I love you like a brother, but I'm a big girl and this," I said, pointing to my bikini, "is just a swim suit. Every girl at the party will be wearing one."

"Yeah, I know. But do you have to wear one like that? It looks like something Maya would wear."

"She is wearing this, just in a different color."

Gabe's jaw about hit the floor when I said that, but he quickly recomposed himself. Then he started to laugh. "You are trying to kill me. Well alright, let's get this thing over with."

Gabe practically didn't leave my side for the remainder of the night – giving death looks to anyone he thought was looking too long. It probably didn't help that Dylan and Ryan started making catcalls and whistling as soon as we made it downstairs.

The party was a lot of fun. Maya had basically invited our entire class, including some of the seniors, most of whom were on our team. Everyone had a great time swimming and hanging out by the pool. There were even a good number of people dancing in the makeshift dance floor Maya had created in the gazebo. She had it cutely decorated with little dangling stars, which she said added to the romantic effect. She really did think of everything.

Once the sun went down, the pool lights turned on at the same time as my mom came out holding a lit birthday cake while everyone sang "happy birthday" to me. When I had blown out the candles, everybody started cheering and Gabe pulled me into a hug as he kissed the top of my head and whispered, "Happy Birthday, Emma."

I was looking around at all the faces that were now chanting "cake" and I couldn't help but feel a little bummed that the one face I really wanted to see never showed up. I knew it was a long shot after the way Maya had invited him, and then there was the fact that I didn't even know him. *But wait, what was I doing? I have got to stop thinking about this boy. Especially since I haven't said one word to him. Like ever.*

I quickly shook that thought out of my head before grabbing a piece of cake for myself. I had only taken two bites when I heard, "Dylan Andrews, you better not!" coming from a giggling but trying to sound serious Maya. "Put me down!"

I looked over my shoulder to the pool just in time to see Dylan tossing Maya in. "Gladly!" I watched as Dylan threw his fist up in the air, making a show out of his triumphant victory. He had just started to walk away from the pool when his eyes found mine. His eyebrow went up as he cocked his head to the side. I looked at him curiously, then he shouted, "Birthday girl next!"

"Oh. No. You. Don't." I hollered, jumping out of the chair I had been sitting in, letting my cake fall to the ground as I made a mad dash around my backyard away from Dylan. Through some sort of primal instinct Ryan and Gabe had joined this game, and now I was being hunted by three of them. I had just turned the corner around the tennis court fence when I saw Ryan coming from that direction. I quickly turned to head back the other way when I face planted into Gabe, who quickly grabbed me and threw me over his shoulder. "Gabriel Shawn Walters, do not even think about throwing me into that pool! I'm finally dry!" I furiously kicked my legs, trying to break free.

"I would never," he countered in a mocking voice walking up to the pool. "I'm jumping in and I'm taking you with me!"

"Eeeek!" I squealed as he jumped in.

As soon as he surfaced, he threw his fist up in the air and all the guys cheered at their ridiculous victory. "Oh you think that was funny do you?" I swam back toward Gabe and dunked him, taking him by surprise. He popped back out of the water and looked at me with a shocked expression before smiling and yelling, "chicken fight," cueing everyone to jump in the pool and partner up.

The party lasted until around eleven thirty. Once the last of the stragglers finally left, Maya and I went back to my room and got ready for bed. In bed Maya rolled over and looked at me. "You bummed prince charming didn't make it tonight?" I told her no and gave her the same excuse I had given myself earlier "that I didn't even know him" then turned over and closed my eyes. Even though I had said it out loud this time, it didn't sound any more true then when I had thought it to myself earlier. What was it about this boy?

Chapter Three

Monday morning came way too soon. To make matters worse, between the tennis tournament, my birthday, and thinking about Jake Reynolds, I had completely forgotten about my history homework that was due today. *What is my issue? This is so not how I need to start this school year.* I was deep in thought, while getting my book out of my locker for my first class, when Maya nudged my shoulder.

"Don't look now, Em," she said, gesturing across the hall.

I glanced up and it took me all of like five seconds to realize what she was talking about. Then, before I could even think about what my legs seemed to be doing all on their own, I was standing right in front of Jake, prompting him and the guy he was with to stop talking and look right at me.

"Hi, I'm Emma," I blurted out, while noticing that his eyes were a piercing shade of blue. Like mesmerizingly blue. A girl could get lost in those sapphires.

Oh God, awkward, think Emma think.

"That, um, was a great game you played with Ryan on Friday," I offered, mortified that I had just walked right over and introduced myself. What was the matter with me? I don't do these kinds of things. I just need to stop while I'm ahead and walk away.

But before I could turn around he said, "I'm Jake and this is Evan," gesturing to the guy he had been talking to. "I see you finally found some clothes," he chuckled. I was about to ask him what exactly he meant by that when I felt Maya loop her arm around mine.

"Yes. Well, would you have rather me worn this to a pool party that you didn't bother attending. I think not. And I see you have traded a blonde for a brunette." Maya gave him a flirty wink.

He looked a little confused at first but must have realized what Maya was getting at. "Oh uh, Maya this is Evan, Evan, Maya."

"Great, now that we all know each other Emma and I had better get to class. Later boys," she said while walking away and taking me with her.

"Oh my gosh, Em! What was that?" Maya asked once we had turned the corner down the hall. "You just march right up to him and start talking? Who are you and what have you done with my best friend?"

"More like freezing. Talking would require words that make sense and form an intelligent sentence," I sighed frustratingly. "I mean, why the heck can't I speak when I get nervous? He probably thinks I am such an idiot!"

"A cute idiot!"

"Oh, please. He seemed annoyed or scared. Definitely not interested."

Just then the warning bell sounded letting everyone know it was time to get to class. I have no idea what we talked about during first period – something about verb tenses. As if I didn't have a hard enough time understanding my Spanish teacher on a normal day. All I could focus on during class was how humiliated I was about what I did, and the rest of the morning went by pretty much the same way. After Spanish was English with Ryan, who always saves me a seat since he gets there before me, next is calculus, then history with Ryan and Maya. Each class was sort of a blur. All I could think about was trudging up to Jake and blurting out my name.

After class, the three of us walked over to the senior parking lot to meet Dylan and Gabe for off-campus lunch. Maya had already filled Ryan in on the events of this morning but hadn't informed Gabe and Dylan since we didn't have any classes with them because they were seniors. Well, Ryan was a senior too, but since he transferred from private school his junior year, it worked out that he had a couple of classes with us. Maya was just about to spill the beans when Jake and two other guys walked by. One was Evan, who I recognized from my public humiliation earlier.

"Hey, Emma. We are going to Taco Villa if you guys want to join," Jake said casually, stopping right in front of me.

"Eer um, yeah, we might see you there," I uttered awkwardly.

"Cool. We'll grab a bigger table just in case then," he replied, like no big deal.

I stood there trying to figure out what just happened as he jogged over to hop in the back of Evan's Jeep. And dang if he didn't even make that look sexy. *Good Lord, I have got to get a grip.* It wasn't until they were driving away that I realized all four of my friends were looking at me questioningly. Maya was the first to speak up.

"Did I miss something between first and fourth period?" she demanded, raising an eyebrow.

"What? No. What are you talking about?" I stammered.

"Really," she said flatly. "You're going to go with that after Jake walked right up to you and asked if we wanted to join them for lunch?" She put both hands on her hips, while keeping both eyes narrowed on me.

"I have no idea what just happened. I hadn't even seen him again until just now," I said, still trying to process everything.

"Again?" Gabe chimed in.

"For the love of God," Ryan exclaimed, "Dylan, do you have your keys with you?" After dangling his keys in

31

the air, Ryan continued, "Great, now everyone get in Dylan's truck and Maya will explain everything on the way to lunch. Emma, where are we going?"

"Anywhere but Taco Villa," I said quickly.

"Roger that. Subway?" Dylan suggested as he started his truck.

After everyone approved, we headed to Subway and Maya filled the other two guys in on what happened this morning.

"Smooth, Em. Real smooth," Dylan joked.

"Oh gee thanks, Dylan. How did you know I wanted you to add your sparkling two cents?"

"Everyone likes my sparkling two cents. I'm Dylan Andrews," he countered with his usual cockiness.

"Seriously, Dylan. One day someone is going to come along and knock you off your high horse."

"Oh there will definitely be knocking," he said suggestively while smiling wildly.

"Oh. My. God. I give up." I threw my head back and rested it on the back of the seat.

The entire car was cracking up as we pulled into Subway. The guys thought it would be funny to reenact the morning over and over again while we ate, causing everyone to laugh harder. Even though Gabe was laughing and participating, I'm pretty sure I saw a pained expression cross his face once or twice throughout the whole ordeal.

After lunch, the afternoon passed quickly. Why was it that when you couldn't wait for something time seemed to pass so slowly, but when you were dreading something it seemed to get there all too quickly? After the way this day had gone, I just knew I was going to run into Jake at practice. I somehow had gone an entire year not realizing we were on the same team, and now I couldn't seem to stop running into him.

As luck would have it, Maya and I had just pulled into the parking lot closer to the tennis courts when Jake walked up. I closed my eyes and prayed he didn't see us.

No such luck.

"So I didn't see you guys at lunch," he said with the same casualness he had used earlier.

Maya gave me a quick glance before saying, "I'm going to go warm up. See ya in a sec." Then she walked toward the courts we always warmed up on.

I turned my attention back to Jake, trying to act as casual as he had, before shrugging. "The guys really wanted Subway."

"Yeah, Subway is good," he said, fidgeting with his tennis racquet.

"Yup." I just knew my face was turning red. This whole thing was so awkward. I was about to say we should get to practice and quickly walk away, but he spoke up again.

"Well, we should probably get to practice, but would you want to hang out for a little while after?" he asked coolly.

"Eeer yeah," was all I could get out before watching him smile and then turn to walk away toward the rest of the team.

I don't know how long I had been standing there trying to process what had just happened for the second time today, when Gabe walked up and asked what that had been all about. He must have seen Jake talking to me. I told him he just wanted to know where we ended up going to lunch. I wasn't about to include the fact that he had asked me to hang out after practice. He apparently must have been satisfied with my answer because he threw his arm around my shoulder and started talking about something that happened in physics as we walked up to the courts.

I couldn't help but notice the grimace on Jake's face when I walked up to the courts with Gabe's arm draped over my shoulder. Gabe must have noticed it too because he tightened his grip as he yelled over to Dylan, who was warming up a couple courts over, to save him a spot. Then he pulled me in and gave me a quick kiss on the lips before jogging over to Dylan's court.

"What the heck, Gabe?" I shouted after him.

Still jogging, he turned around and back trotted as he jokingly yelled, "Don't worry babe, I'll sneak in later." With a grin that stretched from ear to ear, he turned back around and finished jogging over to a very shocked Dylan.

I shot him a look, then stomped over to Maya's court to warm up, making no attempt to hide my irritation. What was going on today? I only got to warm up for about five minutes before coach yelled for us to take a lap and then grab a partner for mixed doubles. Gabe and I always paired up for mixed doubles, but I was still irritated about the little stunt he pulled earlier. So I asked Ryan to play with me instead. But before he said anything he was glancing around, not sure what to say, knowing Gabe and I always played together. I snapped my fingers in his direction, "Ryan Bennet, do not look for Gabe. I can play with someone else if I want to."

"Yeah, but this is kind of y'alls thing and um..."

"It's fine. Today I want to play with you." I snapped as I pulled him over to a court.

"What the hell do you think you're doing, Bennet?" Gabe called out as he was jogging over to our court.

"You really think I'd play with you after that little stunt you pulled?" I stated. "Uhhh no. March yourself over there and find a different partner," I said, shooing him away with my free hand.

After giving me his best plea and pouty face, he realized I was serious and walked away. He ended up partnering with a very excited Michelle. Knowing that he had to play with an annoying sophomore all practice, I couldn't keep from smiling and feeling as though vengeance was mine.

Ryan and I played great all practice, though I couldn't help but miss Gabe. This really was our thing. Not to mention, we usually didn't lose when we played together.

At the end of practice, I was talking to Maya, Dylan, and Ryan by the gate when Gabe walked up behind me and wrapped his arms around my middle. Snuggling his head in my neck he whispered, "Still mad at me?" I shook my head no and felt him smile against my cheek. I was turning to face him when I saw Jake looking over at us with a scowl on his face. Realizing what this must look like, I quickly stepped away from Gabe and stood closer to Maya. Gabe was frowning when Jake walked up.

"We still hanging out?" he asked, glancing over at Gabe.

"Uh, Yeah," I quickly replied. "I just need to put my stuff in my Jeep."

"OK cool, I'll walk with you." he offered.

I could tell Gabe was about to say something. Maya must have sensed it too because she stepped in. "I guess that leaves the four of us. Come on boys one of you is buying me ice cream!" she said in true Maya fashion, practically dragging Gabe along behind her. It didn't take much convincing on Dylan's part, and Ryan was always up for ice cream.

As the four of them were walking away, I turned back to Jake who was gesturing with his hand for me to go first. Neither one of us said anything on the way to my car. I had just opened the back to put my gear in when he asked if he could hop in.

"Uh, sure," was all that came out. *Why couldn't I seem to speak around this guy?* I quickly put my stuff in the back of my Jeep and then walked over to the drivers seat so I could turn on the AC. It was the end of August and we were still dealing with the dry West Texas heat in the high nineties.

"So what do you want to do?" I asked, adjusting my air vents.

"I thought we could just listen to some music and talk for a while if that's OK with you."

"Yeah, sure," I turned the radio to my favorite country station.

Hunter Hayes just started playing when Jake began, "You and Gabe huh? How long have y'all been together?" I couldn't help but pick up on the annoyance in his voice, but on the outside he still had that calm, casual thing going on.

"Oh, we aren't actually together. He's one of my very best friends. I guess I could see why people would think we were together though."

"You guess? The guy freaking kissed you before practice and can't seem to keep his hands off you." he let out, this time not hiding his frustration.

A little shocked at his reaction, it took me a second to respond. And a small smile touched my lips as I realized, he sounded jealous. "Yeah, I was upset with him for that. I don't know why he did that." Not wanting to talk about Gabe and I any longer, I redirected the conversation to him. "So that girl you were with at the mall was really pretty. Is she your girlfriend?" I was trying to sound as nonchalant as possible, but at this point I was just thankful words were coming out.

"That's right, you were at the mall with Maya the other day. No, that was my sister Quinn. We were picking out a gift for our grandmother. Her birthday is a few days after yours. How was your party, by the way?"

"Oh." Great, he barely remembered seeing me at the mall. I clearly don't have the same effect on him that he does on me, but at least he remembered it was my birthday. "It was fun. You know, the usual back to school bash pool party. Maya always mixes up the theme and people actually dress accordingly, even though it's mostly a pool party. Probably because they know she wouldn't let them in if they didn't," I said, laughing to myself.

"Well, actually, I don't know. This was the first time I was ever invited to one of Emma Crawford's "back to school bash" pool parties," he said teasingly.

"Oh," I replied sheepishly. "Well, my birthday just happens to always fall on the first week of school, so Maya sort of turned it into a birthday slash back to school party all in one," I said matter-of-factly. "And I have no control over the invite list." I quickly added before looking away, feeling my cheeks start to turn red and not sure why I suddenly felt the need to defend myself.

He was smiling when I looked up. "What? What's so funny?" I asked, sounding more demanding than I meant to.

Chuckling, he replied, "Nothing. I'm just sorry I didn't get to make it to the party. You'll have to let me take you out some time to make it up to you. Unless you think Gabe would mind."

"I'd like that," I answered a little too quickly. "And Gabe won't mind. I told you we are just friends."

"Whatever you say, Blondie." I noticed as his eyes gazed down to my lips as he spoke, which caused my

38

cheeks to feel warmer than they already did. "I better get going before my parents get any ideas and play fifty questions when I get home. See you tomorrow?"

"Yeah, see you tomorrow." Now I was smiling and blushing. He had just nicknamed me. If anyone else had called me Blondie it would have unnerved me, but I liked the way it sounded when he said it.

"Alright, later." Before I knew what he was doing he leaned in, kissed me on the cheek, then got out and walked toward where he was parked. I sat there stunned as I watched him climb into his truck. Never in my life has any boy had this effect on me – this intense attraction and longing to be near him. He made me feel things I never knew I could feel, and currently all I could think about was that I wish it would have been my lips.

I waited till he pulled out of the parking lot before calling Maya and heading home.

"What? Who kisses someone on the cheek these days?" she practically yelled, not able to hide her excitement.

"It was sweet," I defended, putting my hand to my cheek where he had kissed me, remembering the way his lips had felt against my skin.

"OMG, Em! I can't believe it! So he asked you to hang out again? Like a date? When are you meeting him next?" she squealed.

"No, not like a date. He just said he wanted to make it up to me since he missed my birthday. Besides, he's a senior."

"And? Gabe, Ryan, and Dylan are seniors. It's so a DATE! I'm so excited for you, Em! EEK!"

"OK. Maybe a date. But I don't want to get too excited. He hasn't even officially asked me out yet. I mean, I don't even know when we are going. Oh no! What if he was just being nice? What if..."

"Em, get out of your own head. The boy clearly likes you. Not to mention, I thought Jake and Gabe were going to throw down after Jake asked if y'all were still hanging out after practice."

"I know! I don't know what has gotten into Gabe lately. Thanks for diffusing that earlier."

"No prob. Well, my mom is calling me down for dinner so I'll talk to you later, biatch."

"Mmkay. Later, Maya."

The rest of the week went by pretty much the same way. Jake had asked me to hang out and just talk every day after practice. Gabe wasn't too thrilled about it, but Maya was great at coming up with reasons for her and the boys to leave quickly after practice. By Friday, I was starting to think Jake would never officially ask me out but before practice he pulled me aside.

"Hey, Em," he said seeming more nervous than he had all week. "I was wondering if you were free tonight for me to take you out, to make it up to you for missing your birthday?"

OK breathe, act cool Em. Act cool.

"Yeah, I am. But you don't have to worry about making it up to me," I said sweetly.

40

"OK, well then I was hoping you'd be free to go out with me tonight." He rubbed the back of his neck as he spoke, causing his bicep to flex in the process.

I bit my bottom lip as I tried to focus on my response instead of how the sight of his muscle flexing caused me to be keenly aware that my breathing had turned into slow, deep breaths. "I'd love too. Pick me up at seven?"

His eyes were on my lips when he tried to speak. "Uh, yeah. Seven." The way he looked at me when he finally looked me in the eyes, I could have sworn he was about to kiss me. Much to my disappointment, he simply gestured for me to head to the courts. Didn't even say anything.

All eyes were on us when we finally made it to practice, which caused my cheeks to blush. Maya practically ran over and pulled me onto her court. "He asked you out, didn't he?" she whispered. As soon as I nodded, confirming her suspicion, she shrieked, "I knew it! I could so tell by the way you two looked when y'all walked onto the court together."

"That obvious?" I asked a little nervously.

"Like, Duh," she giggled. "It looked like the two of you wanted to tear each other's clothes off, and like y'all would rather be anywhere but here. If you know what I mean," she concluded with a smirk.

It must have hit us at the same time cause instantly we made eye contact, then glanced over at an apparently unhappy Gabe.

"Ah jeez, looks like you might have your hands full with that one. He has asked me what is up with you and Jake after practice every day this week."

Turning back to her I quickly asked, "What? Maya! Why didn't you tell me?"

"You have been on cloud nine since Monday afternoon, and I was not about to ruin that for you," she snapped. "Besides, he could have asked you himself. I am not about to become the middle man in this love triangle," she giggled as she formed a triangle with her fingers in the air.

"Oh my God!" I laughed, while hitting the ball to the people across the net.

Gabe didn't talk, much less look in my direction, the rest of practice and left as soon as practice was over. I asked Ryan about it when we were getting our stuff together, but he told me not to worry about it and that he'd eventually get over it. I guess Ryan was right. Besides, I couldn't worry about it now, I had a date to get ready for! So I grabbed Maya and we left for my house to get me ready for my date with Jake.

Chapter Four

An hour and a half later, my hair was curled and my makeup was flawless thanks to Maya who was currently spritzing my favorite perfume "in all the right places" according to her. Then, I sat in my bowl chair and watched as she rummaged through my closet, picking out what I should wear on my first date with Jake. After a few no's and one hell no she finally pulled out a top and bottom and said, "Perfect!" It was a pair of white shorts that fit just right and a blue top that hugged all the right places.

"Oh my gosh!" I squealed looking at my outfit in the mirror. "This is perfect. And I didn't even know I had this top."

"Emma, it's sad when you have so many clothes you don't even know what's in there." Maya was gesturing to my closet when we heard someone pulling in the driveway. We looked at each other, then ran to my window and looked down to see Jake turning off his Ford and getting out of his truck. We both instantly backed away from the window. "Somebody's early. Looks like Jakie Poo can't wait to get you in that big ole truck of his," she said, wiggling her eyebrows up and down.

"Oh stop!" I half laughed, whacking her on the arm.

Thirty seconds later, my dad was calling up the stairs, "Emma, your friend is here. Why don't you come on down and introduce me to him," he said sternly.

I rolled my eyes at Maya before turning to head down. On the way out of my bedroom door, Maya slapped my butt and whispered, "Have fun, biatch. Don't do anything I wouldn't do."

I turned back to look at her. "So, basically anything."

She gave me a dramatic wink before shooing me down the stairs. How I loved my best friend.

When I reached the last stair, I heard my dad giving Jake the "she's my daughter, you better treat her with respect speech."

"Daddy, I see you've met Jake," I said, turning the corner of the stairs and walking into the kitchen. Hearing me come in, Jake glanced over in my direction. When our eyes met, he looked me up and down and a huge smile broke across his face, causing me to blush.

My dad turned and gave me an innocent look. "Hey my favorite oldest daughter. Jake and I were just having a little conversation man to man. Isn't that right, Jake?"

"Yes sir, Mr. Crawford." Jake said confidently, looking my dad square in the eye.

I could tell my dad liked Jake already. He always did have a soft spot for a "nice, confident, and respectful young man," as he would say.

"Well if you're done with your conversation, Jake and I will be back later," I teased.

My dad walked up and gave me a hug, then shook Jake's hand before we turned to head for the front door. Jake had just opened the door for us when my dad added, "Jake, be sure and have her home by ten thirty tonight."

Before Jake could respond I had turned around, "Dad?" I was a little embarrassed that it came out more whiney than I intended. "My curfew is midnight. That's an hour and a half earlier than normal." As soon as that came out, I was officially embarrassed. Jake might not even want to hang out that late. What if he wanted to bring me home after dinner? Oh God, I can't believe I just did that.

"Yes, sir. I'll have her home no later than ten thirty, Mr. Crawford." With that, my dad gave him a nod and we were finally out the door.

We walked in silence to the passenger side of his truck. When he opened the door for me there were flowers in my seat. He stepped forward to grab the bouquet before turning back to me and smiling, "These are for you."

A huge smile spread across my face as I took the flowers. "Jake, these are beautiful," I gushed.

"I wasn't sure what your favorite flower was, but the lady at the counter told me I'd be safe with a summer mix," Jake replied a little sheepishly while I smelled my flowers.

45

I was still beaming when I looked up at him. "Well, she was right. These really are lovely and they smell amazing. Let me just run inside and put these in water."

Jake was grinning triumphantly at this point and said he would get the truck started while I ran inside. I quickly walked back to my house to look for a vase. As soon as I walked through the door with flowers, my mom saw me. "Oh, honey, I'm so sad I missed Jake picking you up for your first date. I was back in our room and didn't even hear the doorbell ring." My mom was mid rant when she saw the flowers, "Oh, and he brought flowers! He's a keeper!" she said as she gave me a wink.

I couldn't help but laugh at my mom. "Aren't they beautiful?" I asked excitedly. "Would you mind putting these in water for me so I can get back out to my date?"

"Of course, honey. Have fun tonight."

I thanked my mom then headed back to the door before turning back to add, "By the way, Maya is here. I told her she could stay and get ready before leaving to meet up with the guys."

"OK, thanks for letting me know. But you need to go so you're not keeping that boy waiting any longer."

And with that I was out the door. As soon as Jake saw me, he hopped out of his truck and ran around to open my door. Once he made it back to the driver's side, he looked over at me and smiled, "I hope you like Mexican food."

"It's my favorite. Where are we going?"

Jake told me about a place I had seen countless times but had never been to. Once we parked, Jake insisted that I stay seated so he could run around and open the door for me – again.

When we walked inside, I immediately noticed how quaint this place was. The hostess was down a little hall with two rooms on either side that contained just a handful of tables in each room. There was a small bar area off of one room and what looked like a party room off of the other. It was dimly lit inside, and we were seated at a small table in the corner.

Our waitress was around our age and had striking features with long, dark, almost black, hair that was pulled up into a ponytail. She was pretty but Jake didn't seem to notice, which I could tell aggravated her. She seemed like the type of girl who was used to not having to work hard for a guy's attention. So when she was getting our drink order, glancing at me only long enough to let me know she was talking to me, she shamelessly flirted with Jake. I must say I was a little shocked when she leaned over to touch Jake's arm, revealing her very large cleavage, to let him know she'd be right back with our drinks. She lingered slightly before turning around to head for the kitchen.

"Did that really just happen?" I found myself asking in disbelief.

Jake shrugged. "Guess I just have that effect on women," he teased. "But I don't really care if I have any effect on her."

"Oh, and why is that?"

"I'm already out with the one I want." He looked me directly in the eyes, causing me to blush. I was not used to any guy being so forward and I had to admit, I liked it. "So what do you typically get at Mexican food places?" Jake asked while opening his menu.

"Well, enchiladas are my favorite, but whenever I go somewhere new I like to get a combo plate so I can try several things to see what's good."

Jake looked up at me with a humorous expression on his face. "I take it you're not one of those girls who orders something small, takes two bites, then declares she's full."

I thought about it for a second and realized most girls probably don't eat much on a date. I hadn't really thought about that before, especially since this was my first official date. I mean, I had gone out with guys plenty, but we were always with a group and there was never any pressure of being on a "date".

I let out a small laugh, "Guess not," shrugging as I again felt a blush spread up my cheeks.

"Good, I hate it when girls do that."

Just then our waitress came back with our drinks. Despite the fact that she was practically throwing herself at him while taking our order, Jake kept his eyes on mine, looking up only to hand her his menu. I couldn't help but smile as our waitress rolled her eyes when she said our food should be out shortly, before walking away.

We talked easily through the rest of dinner. I found out that other than tennis, he also plays golf. It sounds like something he and his dad do a lot together. I told him that I'd attempted to play golf before, but that I couldn't seem to actually hit the ball. Given that being able to make contact with the ball is sort of crucial in golf, it didn't take me long to decide that golf wasn't for me.

Jake told me all about his college plans to attend Texas A&M, and I couldn't help but feel excited that we wanted to go to the same school. Then I realized that I was getting a little ahead of myself. After all, this is only our first date. I shouldn't care about things like that. Right?

When we were finished eating, Jake paid for our dinner while gently brushing off another advance form our waitress. This girl really couldn't take a hint. As we were standing up to go, our waitress gave one last attempt to flirt with my date. This time Jake didn't even acknowledge her. He simply reached down, grabbed my hand, and led me out of the restaurant. This caused about a million butterflies to go off in my stomach, and all I could do was smile at our waitress as we walked right past her to the door.

Jake held my hand the entire way out to his car. Just the touch of his hand caused my body to react in a way I was not used to. *Holy crap, what was wrong with me? We are just holding hands. No big deal, right?* He dropped my hand to open the truck door, and I immediately missed his touch. He placed his hand on the small of my back when he stepped back to let me get in. That one little move sent a shiver down my spine, and I could feel the heat rising in my cheeks as I turned around and gave him a shy smile.

I could tell it was affecting him too because of the way he was looking at me and how he stuttered when he tried to speak. He quickly cleared his throat and began again.

"Since I have to have you back by ten thirty, we don't have time to see a movie or anything. So how do you feel about getting some ice cream and going to the park?"

"That sounds great," I offered, while trying to calm the rush of emotions that had presently taken over my body.

* * *

We had been at Baskin Robbins for about ten minutes, and I still had no idea what type of ice cream I was going to get. I was holding four sample spoons and was about to sample the double chocolate fudge when I noticed Jake leaning on the ice cream case starring at me with an amused look on his face.

"What? Picking out an ice cream flavor is a big decision," I said, defending myself. I was unable to control the smile that had taken over my face, which caused Jake to burst out laughing.

"Alright, Blondie, why don't we do this? We will get two large cups of ice cream. You pick which two flavors you want in your cup. I'll get the other two you can't seem to choose between in mine, and we will share."

"Oh my gosh. Really?" I beamed. "But then you wouldn't get to pick your favorite."

50

Noticing my obvious excitement, he gave me that perfect smile of his. "I would gladly sacrifice my own favorite ice cream if it's going to cause you to get this excited." Then he asked which two flavors I wanted before ordering ice cream for us.

As he was ordering, all I could think about was "is this guy for real?" Even Gabe would have told me that it's just ice cream and to hurry and choose. Jake just kept finding ways to make me feel special.

* * *

Jake pulled up to a small park close to where we had gotten ice cream and he, of course, ran around to get my door. It was a cute little park that had a sidewalk that went around the whole thing. Tall willow trees, with branches that brushed across the ground, were around most of its border – hiding its inhabitants in a cloak of green.

We found a bench near a lamppost and sat down to finish eating our ice cream. About every other bite, Jake tilted his cup toward me so I could scoop out a bite before laughing at something else that he said. When we had eaten all that we could, we walked over to a trash can and disposed of what was left of our large cups and then began to stroll around the park. We only made it a few steps before Jake took my hand, again cueing the butterflies in my stomach. Halfway around the park, he asked me if I had ever climbed a tree. When I told him I hadn't, he said that everyone had to climb a tree at some point in their life and led me over to one of the big willows.

He helped me up before climbing up behind me. We settled on a branch that wasn't too high up that allowed me to recline on the trunk of the tree. We talked hidden away from the world under a blanket of leaves that swayed in the light evening breeze. Eventually, Jake looked down to check his watch.

"We have to leave pretty soon so I can have you back on time, but there is something I've been wanting to do since I first saw you tonight in those little white shorts," he said moving closer to me, causing heat to spread through my entire body.

"Oh yeah?" was all I managed to say as my heart began beating faster.

He leaned in until he was inches from my face, placing one of his hands on the tree trunk behind me. Nerves began to surge through me, and I bit my lip in anticipation. He glanced down, and a smile spread across his face as he reached up and ran his thumb across my bottom lip. "Have you ever kissed someone, Emma?"

"Uh huh." I breathed.

"Good, then you know exactly what I'm about to do." With that, he closed the gap between us and kissed me. When I responded, he placed his other hand around my back to pull me closer and deepened the kiss.

When he finally pulled away, my head was spinning. Sure I had kissed a boy before, but I had never been kissed like that. I couldn't keep from smiling, but in that moment I didn't care. It had been a perfect first kiss and besides, the smile on his face seemed to match mine.

"I guess I have to get you home now."

"Guess so."

Jake climbed down the tree first, then helped me down. We walked hand in hand back to his truck, enjoying what was left of a perfect West Texas night.

The drive back to my house seemed to go by way too quickly. I was in no way ready for this night to end. When we pulled into my driveway, we both sat there silently for a minute or two staring out the front window.

"I had better get inside." I said breaking the silence, reaching for the door and pausing to look back at Jake before opening it. "Thanks for tonight. I had a really great time."

"Me too." He took a deep breath in. "Listen, I know I should wait a day or whatever before calling and asking you out again, but I don't think I could wait a couple of days before seeing you again. What are you doing tomorrow?"

I sat there for a few seconds staring at him in disbelief. I mean, I had a great time; I really did. But he's a senior, and I barely know him and he couldn't possibly be that into me. Could he?

"Really? Tomorrow?" I couldn't believe it even as I was saying it out loud. And good grief, what was it about this boy that kept causing me to smile like this?

"Yes, really. What do you say?" He reached over and laced his fingers with mine, running his thumb back and forth across the outline of my hand. That one little move caused me to momentarily forget what I was supposed to be thinking about. I watched his thumb run up the side of mine and then back down and across to the base of my pinky.

Every time he touched me, my body reacted in a way I wasn't quite used to. I was completely focused on what he was doing and had a building desire to lean over and kiss him the way he had kissed me earlier. But before I could lean in, he interrupted my thoughts.

"Emma?" I looked up and met his eyes. I could tell by the look on his face that he was enjoying the affect he had on me.

"Oh, right," I snapped myself back into reality. Was I really about to lean in and kiss him? I've never been so bold with anyone. And is it that I am bolder or is it that my body seems to have a mind of its own when I'm around him. *Good Lord, I need to get it together.*

"Tomorrow afternoon Maya is coming over to lay out. Then the guys are joining us later to hit on the court. You can come if you want." I know he probably wasn't looking to hang out with me and my friends, but I was practically willing him to say yes in my head.

"You have a tennis court in your backyard?"

"Uh...yeah." I laughed. "My dad likes me to practice – a lot. He thinks I'm going to go pro or something one day."

"Awesome. What time should I be here?"

"The guys are coming over around two. So if..."

"Great. I'll see you around two tomorrow then," he jumped in before I could say anything else.

"Sounds good."

I couldn't believe Jake didn't mind coming to hang out with me and my friends. We are just getting to know each other, and he didn't seem phased at all about being thrown in with the whole crew. How easygoing he is just makes me like him that much more.

The porch lights flickered on and we both looked at the clock.

"Holy crap! It's ten forty-five. I better get inside before he comes out here."

"In my defense, I had you here at ten twenty-nine, a whole minute early. And he said nothing about being inside by ten thirty," Jake said jokingly, before running around to open my door. I couldn't stop myself from laughing at the goofy grin all over his face when I hopped out of the truck.

"Goodnight, Jake. I'll see you tomorrow."

"Night, Emma."

He waited till I opened the front door and turned around and waved before climbing back in his truck and driving off. I was prepared for anything my dad was about to say because, frankly, nothing could ruin my mood. I can't believe my first date was so incredibly perfect with a boy who was so incredibly perfect. I hadn't realized that I sighed, out loud, until I heard my dad chuckle.

"The date went well tonight, I take it?"

"Oh, William, leave your daughter alone," my mom said, walking into the room and playfully swatting my father on the arm. "No seventeen-year-old wants to talk to her dad about her first date." Then she turned to look at me, "So let's go upstairs so you can tell me all about it."

My dad burst out laughing, shooing us both upstairs so I could tell my mom about my date with Jake. I told my mom where we went to dinner and what happened with the waitress. She gushed when I told her about how he got two large cups of ice cream because I couldn't make up my mind. I left out the part about the park because I didn't really want to discuss our kiss with my mom. My mom and I have always been close, but that still didn't mean I wanted to go into those kinds of details with her.

"Oh, honey, I am so glad your first date was wonderful! I'm sure you can't wait to tell Maya all about it, so I'll get out of your hair." My mom stood up off my bed and began to leave, pausing when she got to the door, "Night, Em. I really am glad your date went well."

"Thanks. Night, mom."

I wasted no time calling Maya once my mom left. When I told her about the waitress I couldn't keep from laughing when she said, "That bitch!" I told Maya how Jake wouldn't pay any attention to her and how he made a show of grabbing my hand when exiting the restaurant. I waited for her to tell the guys to shut up so she could finish listening to my story. Then, I heard Gabe grumble in the background, shortly followed by a door slamming. Before telling me to go on, Maya told me not to worry about it and that he had been in a bad mood all night. I thought about Gabe briefly but quickly decided that I was not going to let him ruin my good mood and continued telling Maya about my date. She practically screamed when I told her how he kissed me.

"Wow, Em, he is too much. And the way he kissed you, it's like something you'd see in a movie. I was still drooling over the ice cream thing, then you tell me about that. Oh, he's good!"

"I know, right! I don't know what it is about him, but he makes me feel..."

"Horny."

"Maya! Oh my God!"

"I'm just sayin'. I wasn't even there and that boy..."

"Wow. Really? Stop."

Maya busted out laughing.

"So when do you think he'll call you again?" she finally asked, once she had composed herself.

"Actually, he asked if he could see me tomorrow."

"Shut up! What did you say?"

"Well...he may be coming over tomorrow when the boys do."

"Shut up, shut up!" she screamed.

In the background, I heard Ryan yell something about not being able to hear the end of the movie that she was making them watch. I could practically feel her roll her eyes when she said she had better go.

After I hung up with Maya, I went into my bathroom to get ready for bed. As I walked out, my phone beeped. It was a message from Jake saying he couldn't wait to see me tomorrow. I had just texted him back, when my window opened.

"From the smile on your face, I bet I could guess who that was," Gabe said, clearly annoyed.

I tossed my phone on my bed, then folded my arms. "What are you doing here, Gabe? It's late." I couldn't believe he had the nerve to come over and take out his bad mood on me. Even though I was pretty sure I was the cause of it. *Wait. Why am I feeling guilty?*

"Oh, so you get a boyfriend and now you can't hang out with your actual friends?" he uttered harshly, before storming into my bathroom.

"Seriously? Why are you acting like this? And you better keep it down before my parents hear you," I snapped, following him into the bathroom.

"Why am I acting like what?" he shot back.

"Like this, like a dick," I said angrily.

All of a sudden the scowl on Gabe's face softened and a smile threatened his face. "Like a dick?"

First he stormed into my room, then he picked a fight with me, and now he's mocking me and suddenly not angry? "What the heck, Gabe? I can't handle your mood swings tonight."

"Like a dick?" he repeated. This time not trying to hide his smile.

"Yes, like a dick. What could possibly be so funny about that?"

"That's just not something I'd expect to hear coming from you. Maya, yes. But not you."

I thought about it for a second, then let out a small laugh. That was definitely something Maya would say.

58

"Gabe, what are we doing? I don't want to fight with you."

"I don't know. I'm sorry for acting like a 'dick'," he said smiling and stepping closer to me. "Can you forgive me?"

He was giving me his best pouty face, so I threw my hands up in the air. "Fine, but don't you ever barge in here acting like that again," I spoke as sternly as I could.

"Oh yeah?" he challenged with a cocky smirk.

"Yeah," I said matter-of-factly, placing both hands on my hips.

"Well, we'll see about that," he uttered under his breath. Then, before I even realized what was happening, Gabe had me in his arms and was settling down in the bowl chair with me on his lap.

We sat there quietly, just looking at each other for a second. It didn't take long before my mind turned to Jake and our perfect date, and I realized for the first time that neither one of us had bothered to turn the bathroom light on during this entire ordeal. So with just the light from my bedroom creeping in, I sat there with Gabe – with a hint of guilt – as my night replayed through my mind.

"I really am sorry about tonight, Em," he spoke softly, pulling me closer.

"Me too. Let's never do this again, OK?" I nuzzled myself into his neck – again feeling a twinge of guilt. *What? Where was this coming from?* Gabe and I were always like this together. So why was I suddenly feeling weird about it?

"I promise, Em." Then, as he ran his fingers through my hair he whispered, "Never again."

Chapter Five

I woke up to my sister sneaking into my room, startling her when I told her good morning.

"Jeez, Emma. You scared me."

"Sorry. What time is it? And why are you sneaking into my room?" I asked groggily.

"It's after ten and I was going to borrow your tanning lotion. I didn't want to wake you up since you got to bed so late." She raised a brow. "By the way, what time did Gabe end up leaving?" she asked humorously.

"Oh, shut up, Kenzie!" I threw a pillow at her.

Even though she is two years younger than me, McKenzie and I are pretty close. She has always known about Gabe sneaking into my room, but I knew she would never tell our parents, who would totally freak.

She picked up the pillow before climbing onto my bed. "So now that you are awake, how was your date with Jake?" she asked excitedly.

I told my sister about my date while she looked at me dreamily. "I wish Ryan would realize I'm not a little kid anymore and take me on a date as romantic as that," she sighed.

Kenzie has had it bad for Ryan since the day that she met him. And Ryan has always viewed her as the annoying little girl that followed him around. But he is way too sweet to ever let her know that. Instead, he treats her like his own little sister, which drives her crazy. But to an almost eighteen year old, a fifteen year old is a baby.

"Kenz, a senior is going to see a freshman as a kid."

"Really, Emma? Don't go all big sister on me right now, OK?"

"OK, Kenz." I checked my cell for the time. "Why don't we get our swimsuits on and go lay out? Maya will be here any minute now to do exactly that."

"About that, I was going to see if I could borrow one of yours." she said mischievously.

"Sure. Just not my new black one," I countered.

"Em! That's so not fair!" she whined.

"And now I have to wear it so you wont sneak up here and put it on later."

"You said you wouldn't go all big sister on me!"

"I'm sorry, Kenz, but when I know you want to wear it because you know Ryan is going to be here later, I'm going to go all big sister on you."

"Whatever," she didn't bother to try to hide her annoyance. "Can I at least wear the yellow one with the cutouts?"

"Sure. Check the top drawer though. If it's not there it may me dirty."

"Eeeek! You're the best!" she squealed, checking the top drawer. "It's here! Meet ya downstairs. Oh and by the way, mom and dad left us money on the table for food today since they wont be back till late. OK, see ya in a sec!"

All I could do was laugh as she ran to her room to change. We may be sisters, but I swear we are so different. Besides being great at whatever sport she plays, she's brilliant – like all AP, top of her class brilliant – and has this charisma that seems to draw people to her. I'm good at tennis but challenged at every other sport, and I am not going to end up at an Ivy League school like she is. She's definitely the queen bee in her circle of friends. She has always been the type to go after what she wants and right now she wants Ryan. This should be interesting.

As soon as I finished putting my new black swimsuit on, I started to pull my hair up in a ponytail when Maya walked into my room while ending a phone call. "Hey, biatch, you ready to get our tan on?" she called out while walking to my bathroom. When she got to my bathroom, she took one look at my black swimsuit and faked wiping away a tear. "I am so proud...I have taught you well, little Emmie."

"What are you talking about?" I looked at my best friend like she was crazy.

"What? Like you didn't wear that swimsuit on purpose because Jake is coming over later."

"Oh crap!" I panicked. "Is this going to make me look like I'm trying too hard?"

Maya looked amused. "You really didn't mean to do this on purpose? Oh well. You're still rocking it. And I don't know why you're worried. You wore it to your party thinking he would be there."

"No, I didn't do this on purpose. I was trying to prevent Kenzie from wearing it. She was planning on parading around in front of Ryan. And good point."

"Gotta hand it to little Crawford. That girl has balls."

I just shook my head as we headed down to the pool. The three of us laid out for a while until we decided that we were hungry. We had just gotten back outside with our snacks when the boys showed up. Early. Typical.

I hadn't really thought about today being weird with Gabe until he got here. And it was weird. Luckily, Maya was distracted with Dylan. A little too distracted. I would have to ask her about that later but was thankful for the distraction at the present. Hopefully, now she wouldn't pick up on me and Gabe. My sister, on the other hand, was completely focused on getting Ryan's attention, so this could be good. Maybe no one would notice.

When Gabe saw that Maya and Dylan were completely captivated with each other and Ryan was busy trying to convince my little sister he just wanted to lay by the pool and listen to his music, Gabe walked over to me.

"Hey, Em," he said wrapping me up in a bear hug like he always does. "So, are we just going to swim or are we actually going to play tennis?" he asked, glancing around at everyone else.

"Doesn't really look like they're up for tennis, does it?" I said, putting my hands on my hips, evaluating the situation.

"Swimming it is!" Gabe exclaimed, scooping me up and jumping in the pool.

When I popped back up, I noticed Gabe had swum to the other side of the deep end. I quickly swam over toward his direction. This means war. "Gabe, I bet you think you are so funny," I called out once I was closer to where he was.

"Not too fast princess, you don't want to pull a muscle."

Oh, it was definitely on. When I finally got to where Gabe was, I threw all my weight into dunking him. As he went down, I had the thought that he went under way too easy. But before I could swim away, he had both my legs and was pulling me under with him.

This time, when we surfaced, we were both out of breath. I looked up to see Ryan yelling "fore" while tossing a float in our direction and then jumping in himself. Gabe grabbed the float and then made sure I could grab on before moving closer to me.

"Emma, about last night..." he began, at the same time my sister jumped in the pool, practically on top of us.

"What the heck, Kenz?"

My sister looked at me and then toward the house. I followed her gaze and saw Jake walking out toward us.

Oh crap! Oh crap! This probably looks so bad.

I quickly swam closer to my sister who mouthed "you're welcome". I gave an appreciative smile. The last thing I want to do is complicate the me, Jake, and Gabe situation. Then I realized it's probably not a good thing if I have a "situation" in the first place. How did I get here?

I swam over to the edge of the pool as Jake walked up holding his tennis racquet. He came ready to play tennis. It never occurred to me to tell him to wear or bring swim trunks just in case. The guys just always have.

"Hey, Jake. Sorry, I didn't think to tell you to bring a swimsuit," I nervously bit my lip.

"No problem. I can just swim in my shorts."

"OK great," I smiled, wondering what he saw when he walked up. Hoping he didn't get the wrong idea, because there wasn't a wrong idea to get. So why do I keep feeling guilty for interacting with Gabe like I always have? When the heck did this get all complicated?

Just then I noticed a very smiley Maya and Dylan walking toward us from the gazebo. Oh, she definitely has some explaining to do. She looked over at me, and I looked at her questioningly. Then she looked over at Jake and her jaw fell open.

I looked back in his direction to see that he had put his racquet on the table and had pulled off his shirt. Holy crap! That boy looked like he had just stepped out of an Abercrombie & Fitch magazine. When I managed to pull my eyes off of him and look back over at Maya, who was now at the pool herself, she mouthed "damn". All I could do was nod my head in agreement. I had just turned back toward Jake's direction when he jumped in and pulled me over to him.

"I'll make sure I bring a suit with me from now on," he whispered, wrapping his arms around my waist.

The feeling of his skin on my skin sent a shiver down my spine, and my body broke out in goose bumps. I was silently praying that Jake wouldn't notice my body betraying me, but the look on his face said otherwise.

"I really am sorry, Jake. I didn't even think to mention that we might swim."

"Trust me. There is never a reason to apologize if it means you in a bikini," he said huskily.

"Oh." He had been here for all of five minutes and I was already blushing.

I had completely forgotten about Gabe until he swam up right next to us. He must have noticed my now red cheeks because he cocked his head to the side and raised one of his eyebrows at me before turning to Jake.

"Hey man, glad you could make it," Gabe said, offering a fist.

"Glad to be here," Jake responded while bumping fists with Gabe.

After their little interaction, Gabe looked at me and winked before swimming off toward Kenzie. I was officially confused. I was not expecting Gabe to go from pissed about Jake to starting a bromance with him. What the heck? And what was he about to say before Jake walked up? He is going to give me whiplash from his mood swings if he keeps this up.

"So who is that with Gabe?" Jake asked, nodding toward Gabe and Kenzie.

"Oh, that's my little sister McKenzie."

"Little sister?" he asked in disbelief.

I wasn't surprised when Jake was shocked Kenzie was my little sister. I even think she looks older than she is. People are always assuming that I am the little sister. Kenzie may be fifteen, but thanks to her long legs, C cup boobs, and overall killer figure she definitely looks like she's in high school. Now add platinum blonde hair and bright green eyes to the equation, and you can see why she's never had trouble wrapping guys around that tan little finger of hers.

"Yes. Little sister. She's only fifteen. So pick that jaw up, mister," I informed, pointing my finger at him.

"Hey now. There is no jaw to pick up. I just would have never guessed she was fifteen," he said, throwing his arms back innocently.

"Whatever," I let out a small laugh and rolled my eyes at him.

"And were you scolding me, Miss Crawford?" There was a playfulness in his voice, as he was once again closing the gap between us.

"Do I have reason to scold you?" I teased.

Jake leaned in close enough for me to feel his breath on my neck. "Oh, I can be a Very. Bad. Boy." Then

68

he scooped me up, cradled me in his arms, and took a squealing me under.

We spent the rest of the afternoon in the pool. Once we were all way past pruney, we decided to lay out so we could dry off, and the boys declared that they were starving. As soon as they were caught up debating what type of pizza we should order for dinner, I rolled closer to Maya.

"Care to share what is up with you and Dylan?" I whispered.

"Please. There is nothing going on with me and Dylan," she said dismissively, waiving her hand in the air.

I pushed up onto my stomach and gave her an "I know you're full of it" look. "Really? You disappear earlier and come back all smiles and giggles. And you haven't been further than two feet apart all day. You really want to stick with that story?" I questioned.

"Shhh. Hot damn, Em. Lower your voice. OK, so there may be something, but it's too early to tell and I don't want to jinx it. OK?" She gave me a pleading look, and I knew she had it bad. My best friend doesn't do serious or relationships. For her to be acting like this was saying something. "And he may have kissed me behind the gazebo."

"Eeeeek!" I squealed as I jumped up into a seated position. Apparently I squealed louder than I meant to because all the guys instantly looked over at us. It was obvious that Dylan knew exactly what I was squealing about because he immediately looked at Maya, who just shrugged at him. Smiling, Dylan shook his head at us, then the boys returned to their conversation about dinner.

"Oh my God! Spill! Don't leave out anything!"

Maya gushed about how he pulled her behind the gazebo and told her that if she was going to keep wearing bikinis like this, he wasn't going to try and hide his feelings anymore and then kissed her. Leave it to Maya to be subtle. Apparently after, she told him "it's about damn time" and so he kissed her again. Then they walked back over to join the group.

"That definitely explains the look on y'alls faces when you guys were walking over here," I laughed.

"Shhh, here they come and I don't think Dylan said anything to the guys yet."

I turned around to see the guys walking over to us. Ryan approached first, asking if we had seen his headphones.

"Those headphones?" I asked, pointing at Kenzie who was listening to music with her eyes closed.

"Son of a bitch," Ryan mumbled.

A clearly frustrated Ryan walked over to Kenzie while the other guys sat down to run their dinner idea by us. Jake pulled me between his legs and reclined me back onto him as he wrapped his arms around my waist, while Dylan ran the different pizza topping options off.

Maya didn't miss a beat saying that she didn't care what they ordered as long as they ordered a cheese as well. I seconded that opinion, causing Jake to fake surprise at how easily I chose what pizza I wanted when there were so many topping options.

"You took her to get ice cream, didn't you?" Gabe joked.

They fist bumped again and broke out in a knowing laugh. It was a little weird how Gabe was all of a sudden just OK today about Jake and I. I mean I was glad because I didn't want things to be weird or complicated. I just wasn't expecting this, I guess.

"What can I say? Choosing an ice cream flavor is a big decision. And besides, Jake here saved the day." I turned around to smile at Jake who took the opportunity to give me a quick peck on the lips.

"Sure did," he said triumphantly. "We got all four of the flavors in question and shared." He squeezed me a little tighter to him, and I thought I saw a defeated look on Gabe's face. But I couldn't be sure because, at that moment, we were interrupted by an irritated Kenzie and Ryan.

"Whatever, I didn't want to listen to your stupid music anyway!" Kenzie shouted before shoving Ryan's headphones back at him and stomping away in our direction.

"Good! Cause this is my stuff!" Ryan huffed.

I don't know what has gotten into Ryan today. Actually, make that here lately. Kenzie has always seriously crushed on him. He used to be very sweet about it, but ever since she has been back from camp this summer he has seemed to be increasingly more hostile and annoyed with her.

"Sexual tension?" Jake whispered in my ear.

"Please. Ryan views her as an annoying little sister. She's fifteen, remember?" I whispered back.

"Whatever you say, Blondie," he teased.

Sure, things have been different between them lately, but it couldn't possibly be because Ryan was into my sister could it? I mean, she is only fifteen. I thought about it for a second longer, then pushed it out of my mind. There was no way Ryan looked at her like that.

When my sister approached us, she asked if I would please tell Ryan to leave her alone because she was no longer speaking to him. She threw one more scowl in Ryan's direction, then stormed off to the house. When she was gone, Ryan finally walked over and sat with us.

"What did you do to her?" Dylan scoffed.

"Nothing. She has just been exceptionally bitchy here lately," Ryan snapped back.

"Whoa bro...chill man. Just chill," Dylan let out in a sarcastic tone trying to diffuse the situation.

"And don't you two look awfully cozy?" Ryan said harshly, looking at Jake and me.

"Seriously, Ryan? You're upset at my sister. That doesn't mean you have to be a dick to me."

Ryan was about to say something else but was interrupted by Gabe laughing to himself. Realizing everyone was now looking at him, he shrugged at us.

"Sorry, I find it amusing that, that is her new favorite word. I thought it was reserved just for me. Apparently not," He said popping his P and his T.

"What?" Maya chimed in, "Em never says stuff like that. And we always hang out together, so when would she have." She stopped mid sentence, realizing exactly when I would have said something like that to Gabe.

Everyone else knew that since the beginning of last year Gabe had made it a habit of climbing through my window. That is everyone except my new boyfriend or whatever he is. We all sort of looked around in awkward silence until Maya spoke up again.

"So who's going to order the pizza?"

"Wait? Am I missing something here?" Jake asked a little uncomfortably.

"Nope. Unless you didn't know Gabe here snuck into Emma's bedroom window just about every night," Dylan informed with a shit eating grin on his face, cueing both Gabe and I to shoot him a look at the same time. "Sorry. Guess you didn't know."

I just sat there. I didn't know if I should move, say something, or what to do. So I sat there. I mean, how do you explain to the guy you just went on a date with that it is in no way how it sounds. Stupid Dylan.

"Dylan, sometimes you can be such an ass," Maya shot out before standing up. "Come on, Em, you and I will go inside and order the pizza while the boys act like children," she spat while shooting Dylan a look.

Maya had just started to order the pizza when Jake walked in the house.

"Hey, Blondie. Can we talk for a sec?" he asked nervously, scratching the back of his head.

"Uh, yeah. We can go up to my room. It's the one on the left," I offered. Jake turned around and headed for the stairs as I looked back at Maya. She had a concerned look on her face, while trying to force a smile.

When we walked in my room, we both stood there silently for a second looking everywhere but at each other.

"So listen," Jake finally said, "I don't want to be that guy you know? So if there is something going on between you and Gabe, just tell me." He let out a frustrated groan. "Look, I don't want there to be, and I know I don't really have a place to even say that. There's just something about you, Emma. I can't explain it. I know I barely know you and this sounds crazy." He stopped for a moment, his jaw clenching as he ran his hand through that tousled, deep brown hair of his. He looked at me with those piercing blue eyes and then took a step closer and grabbed my hand. "Emma, just say the word and I'll step back."

I didn't even have to think about it. I'm not saying I've never thought about Gabe and I before, but he is one of my closest friends. Besides, with Jake it is different. He can make my heart beat faster just by being in the same room. One look from him and I am suddenly aware of every nerve ending in my body. At that moment, I knew one thing for sure. I did not want Jake to step back. In fact, all I really wanted was for him to press his lips into mine.

"I don't want you to step back. Yes, Gabe crawls through my window sometimes. He is one of my best friends, but that's it."

That must have been all he needed to hear. Before I could say anything else, Jake took another step forward, closing the gap between us, and kissed me. I was completely lost in his kiss and didn't even think about the fact that we were standing in the middle of my room with the door open.

"Oh, shit. Um, sorry." I looked up to see Maya with her hand over her mouth trying to back out of my doorway. Jake and I took a step back, looked at Maya, and then looked at each other. Both of us were wearing the same stupid grin. "Oh crap. Sorry you guys. I wasn't even thinking."

"It's fine, Maya," Jake said kindly. "Emma and I were just leaving anyway." He looked over at me with that perfect smile.

"Right. Well. Then I will see you guys outside."

As soon as Maya was out my door, Jake turned to me, "After you." He gestured with his hand for me to go first. When I went to take a step forward, Jake grabbed my hand and pulled me back toward him. "Wait. One more thing." Jake crashed his lips into mine for a second time before stepping back with a smile that reached both of his ears. "Now you can go."

"Oh that's how this works, is it?" I asked slightly breathless.

"Yeah," he uttered in a low, commanding tone. "Would you like me to show you again?"

"As much as I would like to say yes, everyone is going to start to wonder what happened to us."

"Alright. I will just have to steal you away again later."

"I'm counting on it," I said as sultry as I could, then turned to walk out my door.

"Are you flirting with me, Miss Crawford?" he teased.

I stopped and whipped around to look at him, placing a hand on my hip. "I would never."

"Oh, we'll see about that." He lunged forward and with one quick motion threw me over his shoulder. Despite my attempts to wiggle free, he carried me like that all the way outside where we rejoined the group.

When Maya saw us coming she yelled "Ow ow," then slapped my butt before he put me down. "So what happened to the two of you?" she asked innocently.

"Got lost." Jake shot back with a wink.

"It's official. He's a keeper, Em," Maya joked.

"Oh good Lord." He was just as bad as she was. "Maya, looks like you might have met your match," I giggled.

"Hell yeah," she exclaimed. "That's why he's a keeper."

* * *

76

When the pizza got here, Ryan and Gabe brought it and some drinks out to the gazebo. Maya made sure that she and I grabbed what we wanted before she let them unleash on what was left.

By the time we were done eating, the sun had gone down. The guys decided to build a fire in the fire pit, even though it was still like ninety degrees outside. Dylan was hell bent on making s'mores. I never understood why he liked those things so much.

"I just realized I kinda hijacked your day. Hope I didn't ruin any of your plans or anything," I said, turning to Jake as he sat back down beside me.

"Even if I had plans, I would have changed them if it meant getting to spend all day with a sexy blonde in a black bikini."

"Oh, your good."

"That's what they tell me."

"They?" I questioned.

"OK, that's what you tell me," he said before pulling me over onto his lap. "Speaking of you, do you know what I would like to do with you right now?" he asked mischievously.

"Do I want to know that answer?" I challenged.

"Well," he said, standing up with me in his arms, "You're going to find out the answer."

"Oh, no. Don't even think about it."

"What?" he asked innocently. "You're not afraid of a little night swim are you?"

"Maya!" I yelled. "Help!"

77

"Bye, Em. Have fun!" she called back.

"Traitor!"

Maya laughing was the last thing I heard before I hit the water.

"Holy crap the water is cold!" I shouted when I surfaced.

"Some might say refreshing," Jake countered.

"Well, some would be wrong," I stated while swimming to where I could touch.

"Is that so?"

I could hear Jake swimming behind me and stopped to face him as soon as I could touch the bottom.

"Yes. Because this water is freaking cold."

"You didn't seem to mind this afternoon." He raised a brow, then cocked his head to the side.

"You think you are being so cute, don't you?"

"Well, that depends," he said, placing his hands on my hips, causing a million different goose bumps to surface. Stupid betraying body. "Is it working?"

"I just don't know yet." I was trying my best not to let him know he was affecting me, but when he was this close, touching me, it was hard to even talk normal.

"How about now?" he took another step closer, closing the gap between us. I shivered in his arms, and a satisfied smirk broke across his face as he bent down and kissed me. "Emma," he breathed with his forehead pressed to mine. "Something about you makes me crazy. I haven't been able to stop thinking about you since I met you. I don't want to sound lame, but I don't want there to be any question."

"Question?" I gazed up at Jake, not exactly sure what he was saying.

"Emma, will you be my girlfriend?"

A smile spread across my face. "Jake, of course I'll be your girlfriend."

Jake instantly wrapped both arms tightly around me before jumping us backward into the deep end while shouting triumphantly. We were both laughing and splashing the other when Maya and Dylan walked up.

"What the heck is going on over here?" Maya asked.

Jake looked over at her and shrugged. "She said yes," he responded coolly.

"Again...what?" Maya looked from him to me, clearly confused.

I burst out laughing. "I said I would be his girlfriend!"

"Aahhh!" Maya screamed as she jumped in the pool, which caused me to laugh even harder and cueing everyone else to come over to the pool.

We spent the rest of the night swimming and hanging out in the water. I didn't want the night to end.

* * *

Around eleven thirty everyone was walking out to their cars to go home. I walked Jake out to his truck. When he opened the door, he reclined back on his seat and pulled

79

me into him. "Call you tomorrow?" he asked, putting a loose piece of hair behind my ear.

"Sounds good," I smiled, placing my hands on his chest.

"Night, Emma," he reached up, grasping my cheeks with both hands before kissing me.

"Goodnight, Jake," I let out slightly breathless.

That cute smirk spread across his face before he shut the door and drove away.

"Damn, girl! That boy makes me hot just watching you two," Maya exclaimed, breaking me out of my trance.

"Tell me about it," I said pretending to fan myself. "But seriously...I'm tired."

"I bet you are," she laughed. "Alright biatch, let's go get some sleep."

Chapter Six

The next week things couldn't have been any better. Well, except for with McKenzie, who was in what seemed like a constant bad mood since her spat with Ryan over the weekend. Jake started walking me to class whenever his schedule allowed it. It always makes me smile to see him standing there whenever I walk out of class, and I love walking down the hall with his arm over my shoulder. He mixes so well with my friends; you would swear they had been friends forever. He can even keep up with, or should I say, handle Maya.

Friday morning I could hardly wait till the end of the day so I could go out with Jake, even though I was practically going to be with him all day anyway. It was the second tennis tournament of the year. The tournament was at a local community college, which I loved because we got to miss an entire day of school; then we were already in town, so we could still go out that night.

I met Jake's mom in between my matches when I went to cheer for him and Ryan. It was a little awkward introducing myself to my new boyfriend's mom without him there, but she was sweet and easy to talk to. She struck me as the type of person who had never met a stranger. She had big, shoulder-length hair that was the same blonde as his sister's and the biggest freaking ring I have ever seen. Apparently this woman liked her bling because she wore stacked bracelets with different colored jewels and big chunky diamond studs, with enough personality to match all of it. She was just so quintessential Texas glam.

On the other hand, it was extremely awkward to hear how he was conceived only ten minutes after meeting her. I had never met someone who was so bluntly honest and open about the little details of their life with someone who they had just met. By the end of our conversation, it felt like I had known her my whole life.

I couldn't keep from smiling thinking about what Jake would say when I told him that I heard he was a mountain baby and that apparently "all you need to stay warm is a handle of Southern Comfort and a big blanket by the fire." Of course I would finish by adding a big, dramatic wink like she did. Yep, I definitely liked his mom.

After my last match of the day, I found out Dylan had lost his match and that there was a problem. Apparently, he and the guy from the other team, whose name I learned was Talen, already had issues. When they found out they would be playing each other, the trash talk started. At one point during their match, the coaches had to intervene and tell them to play or get off the court. Gabe said it was bad and that once Dylan had lost, he picked a fight with the guy behind one of the courts. Luckily, some guys from our team, including Gabe, saw it happening and pulled them apart before any of the coaches saw. Gabe was usually pretty good at calming Dylan down when he got heated, but for some reason this guy really got to Dylan.

Dylan had always been kind of a hothead but usually cooled down just as quickly as he got mad. Therefore, none of us gave it a second thought once they had been pulled apart. Plus, we were all busy finalizing plans for the night.

Jake had invited me to go to a party one of his friends was throwing at a ranch right outside of town and said I could invite whoever I wanted. So before we left the courts, we all decided to meet there later tonight. I told Maya that Jake was picking me up so she could make plans to ride with one of the guys. Dylan, who still seemed a little rattled, spoke up quickly saying he would grab her on his way. Maya shot me a quick smile before playing it off like it was no big deal, and then we all left to go get ready.

* * *

I was finishing my makeup when my mom walked in and asked if I would be eating with them before I went out. I let her know Jake and I were going to grab food before we met up with everyone else. Satisfied, she smiled and turned to walk out of my bathroom but stopped at the door. "Hey, honey, do you have any idea what has been wrong with Kenzie here lately? She's been a little snippy, don't ya think?"

I set my makeup brush down and turned to face my mom. "Oh, she's just in a bad mood because she has it bad for Ryan, and he made sure she knew he didn't think of her that way."

"Kenzie always has had a thing for Ryan, hasn't she. I wish she would just find a boy her own age to like. Oh well," my mom said as she let out a breath. "But, honey, will you try to talk to her about it. I think she could use her big sister right now."

"Sure, mom. I'll talk to her tomorrow." I picked up my mascara. My mom gave me a smile, then went downstairs to fix dinner for the three of them.

I was downstairs talking with my family, who was eating dinner, when the doorbell rang. I practically ran to the door, composing myself before I opened it.

"Hey, Em. These are for you," Jake said with that perfect smile of his as he handed me a bouquet of flowers. "I hope you like roses."

"Jake!" I gushed. "These are beautiful. We're not even going on a date, date. You are so thoughtful. You seriously spoil me," I blurted out, before quickly making myself stop talking before I said anything else. Realizing that I was rambling and that my entire family was listening to the whole thing, caused my cheeks to turn a bright shade of red.

Jake, I could tell, was loving every minute of it. "You're welcome." Stepping a little closer, he whispered, "And I will always spoil you," then continued into my house. Noticing that I was still standing by the front door, he shrugged, "What? I figured you would want to put them in water."

"Well, yeah," I walked past him into the kitchen to get a vase.

Jake followed behind me and stopped when he saw my family. "Mrs. Crawford, Mr.Crawford," he said, gesturing toward them with a head nod, cueing my sister to clear her throat. "And, McKenzie. Don't worry; I was going to say hi to you too," he teased.

"Well hello to you too, Jake. And what will you and my sister be doing this evening?" she said in her best parenting voice.

"I'm taking her to go eat and then we are meeting up with some of my friends."

"And where will you be meeting up with your friends?" she continued, glancing over at me, laughing when she saw I was giving her a look that said stop talking.

"At my friends ranch right outside of town," he returned kindly. "We usually shoot varmints, and I thought I could teach Emma how to shoot a gun," he said now looking at my dad. "If that's alright with you, sir."

"Jake, do you know how to handle a gun?" my dad asked.

85

"Yes, sir. Been hunting with my father since I could walk. My dad always says that "a safe gun is one you know how to use and are not afraid of."

"Alright then. Just make sure there is no goofing off while holding a firearm, son."

"Yes sir, Mr. Crawford. And what time should I have Emma home tonight?"

My dad looked over at my mom who raised one eyebrow, then turned back to Jake, "Normal curfew is fine tonight. Have fun kids."

We said goodbye to my family, and as we were walking out of the house we heard Kenzie say, "We shoot varmints," followed by my mother shushing her, which caused us both to laugh.

* * *

By the time we got out to the ranch, the sun had begun to go down and a lot of people were already there.

"It's getting too dark to learn how to shoot a gun, and there are way too many people around," he said seriously.

"There is still plenty of daylight," I countered, looking forward to learning how to shoot.

He reached over and placed a hand on my leg, which almost caused me to miss what he was saying, because all I could focus on was how his touch felt. "I take gun safety serious, Emma. When I teach you how to shoot, we will have plenty of daylight and there will not be this many

86

people around. I should have known better than to think I could teach you tonight," he said, still sounding very serious.

"But you will teach me?" I questioned, bummed that I wouldn't be learning tonight.

"Oh, my girlfriend will know how to shoot a gun," this time sounding more playful while sliding over to me. "There is something sexy about a girl who knows how to handle a firearm."

"Is that so?" I challenged, not being able to resist teasing him right back.

"Absolutely," he murmured while bending down to kiss me. We both jumped when someone hit the hood of his truck. Jake looked up to see who it was and then turned back to me with a shit eating grin on his face. "Alright, Blondie, let's go introduce you to everyone."

"What is that look for?" I asked, reaching for the door.

"I'm about to introduce my smokin' hot girlfriend to all my friends." With that, he was out the door and walking around to where I had hopped out. He gave me one of his perfect smiles, then grabbed my hand and led me over to where his friends were standing.

"Jake. Glad you could make it," Evan began, giving Jake a high-five as we walked up. "And I see you brought your friend. What was it again? Gemma?" he asked dramatically, scrunching his face.

"Actually, it's Emma."

"I'm just messing with you," Evan laughed out. "We have all known your name for a while now. Don't know how we couldn't with Jake over here "Emma this" and "Emma that"."

"Whatever man, you're just jealous that you don't have a smokin' hot girlfriend." Jake was wearing a massive smile as he shot me a wink, causing my insides to warm.

"After tonight, that may be a different story," he joked, sliding his arm over my shoulder.

"Yeah Jake, who knows? After tonight I just may fall for all of this," I laughed.

"Well then, darlin', I didn't mean to be rude. Let me introduce you to my friends," Evan played along, turning up his southern charm.

"Hey now. Don't go throwing around darlin's; that's an unfair advantage," Jake pretended to be worried.

I looked over at Jake, cueing him to throw his hands in the air and look at me with that perfect smile. "Naw, I'm serious. He says darlin' with that southern drawl of his and the ladies go crazy every time."

"Ladies?" I teased, looking back at Evan who shot me a wink.

"Worked on you, didn't it, darlin'?" Evan replied, emphasizing his southern drawl this time. "Bet I got you all hot and bothered, if you know what I mean," he said suggestively, wiggling his eyebrows.

"Oh. My. God." I looked at Jake who looked slightly pissed then I burst out laughing. "If I thought Maya met her match with you, I can't wait till she meets this guy." I threw my elbow in Evan's side just hard enough to cause him to retract his arm from around my shoulders, then walked over to a now all smiles Jake. Once Jake had wrapped his arms around my waist I looked back over at Evan, who I couldn't tell was smiling approvingly or checking me out. "I thought you didn't want to be rude," I said, gesturing over to his friends.

"Oh, right. Emma, this is Brody, Heath, and Spencer."

"Nice to meet you guys." They all nodded.

"Hey, biatch," I heard Maya say as she walked up behind me.

"Maya, you're just in time. I was just getting to know Jake's friends."

"So this is Maya," Evan chimed in.

Maya smirked as she turned to face Evan, "So you've heard of me."

I glanced up at Jake and just shook my head. Maya could make anything sound sexy and had clearly piqued Evan's interest. Though at this point I was beginning to think that anything female that moves could pique Evan's interest.

"Actually, we've met before." Maya looked a little confused and then Evan continued, "At school. Emma here had just introduced herself to Jake and then you walked up."

"That's right. You were the brunette with Jake. Lovely to meet you again..."

"Evan."

"Right. Well, lovely to meet you again, Evan."

"Where's Dylan, Maya? Didn't y'all ride together?" I asked, just realizing that Maya walked up by herself.

"When we got here, I said I was going to go find you and he was supposed to be getting us drinks."

"Speak of the devil," Jake said as Dylan walked up with two beers.

"Hey, Reynolds," Dylan replied a little tense, while handing a beer over to Maya.

Noticing the tension, I leaned over to Maya. "What's up with Dylan?" I whispered.

"He is still all worked up about that Talen guy for some reason."

"Really? Why?"

Maya looked as confused as I was and just shrugged her shoulders.

Noticing the obvious tension, Jake suggested the rest of us go find a drink as well. Everyone quickly complied.

"What's with the face?" Jake asked as we walked up to where the drinks were.

"I, uh. Well, how in the world did a high school kid get so much booze?" My cheeks flushed because I knew that was a stupid question as soon as it came out. But seriously, out of every party I have ever been to, I have never seen this much alcohol. I guess I just wasn't expecting this.

Jake laughed, "Older siblings, fake IDs, the usual."

"The usual, huh? So what's your usual?"

"Actually, I don't drink much anymore. I'm typically the designated driver these days, but tonight I made sure the guys set up another ride so I could chauffeur this cute blonde around."

I had to admit I was glad Jake said he wasn't much of a drinker. Not that I would have been mad if he was, but there was just something about it that I liked.

"Cute blonde, huh? Anybody I know?"

"Oh, she's about your height, has that same adorable smile, and, come to think of it, looks exactly like...that girl over there."

I gave him a playful shove. "Oh I bet you think you are pretty funny huh?"

"Yeah, actually, I do," Jake smiled, while pulling me into his arms. "Now what can I get you?"

"Is there a soda anywhere? I don't drink much either. Well, honestly, I've never actually had a drink," I admitted.

"Two cokes it is then," Jake said, popping the lid of the cooler up and grabbing two coke cans.

"Watch out. That's a strong drink you have there," Evan joked. "Don't tell me Emma over here doesn't drink either."

I just smiled and shook my head as I enjoyed the first crisp taste of my coke.

"Nope. Not even a little. And it's not because I haven't tried, cause believe me I have," Maya chimed in.

"How would I ever be able to keep you in line and out of all that trouble if I was drunk too?" I asked dramatically.

"Good point. I'll drink to that," Maya laughed.

"Cheers," Evan said holding out his cup, "To trouble."

"To trouble," Maya exclaimed then quickly downed the rest of her drink. "Who wants to get this girl another drank?"

"Yes! Now that's a girl who's here to party. Allow me, madam," Evan replied, bowing before going to grab Maya another drink.

"Whatever. I'm out of here," Dylan grumbled before snatching another drink himself and walking away.

I could tell that Dylan walking away bothered Maya, but she quickly recomposed herself and shouted something about being ready to have a good time. I watched as she organized a group of people to play a drinking game. As she was explaining the rules to everyone, I knew this night was going to end up with me taking care of Maya. She was annoyingly predictable that way. An upset Maya plus alcohol always equals me taking care of her drunken self.

It has been this way since the beginning of last year. Maya's dad had always been a jerk, but sometime last summer he decided to step it up a notch. The first time we hung out with the guys and they brought beer, Maya's dad had torn into her before she left the house; so, she decided she should try her first beer. Once she popped open the can, she held it up and said, "To you, Dad. Now I can be

92

just like you." That night ended in lots of tears and Maya puking her guts out.

I knew there would be no reasoning with Maya at this point. She was upset about Dylan and had already had a few drinks. I decided I had to find Dylan and try to talk some sense into him if I didn't want to be holding her hair back all night. When I told Jake I was going to find Dylan, he grabbed my hand and said, "Let's go then."

We spent what felt like forever looking for Dylan and never found him. Jake suggested we go check to see if he had wandered back over to Maya. So we walked back over to where Maya still had a group of people playing some other drinking game she had thought up. We quickly realized Dylan was still MIA but found Ryan and Gabe standing around drinking a beer watching the whole ordeal. When they saw us, they both gave me a knowing look.

"Why is Maya shitfaced, and why do I feel like I need to tell Evan to back the hell off?" Gabe asked.

"Good Lord. I don't even know exactly what happened tonight. All I know is Maya seemed off when she first got here, Dylan has been in a pissy mood all day because of the guy from earlier, and something must have happened between the two of them because there was some awkward tension followed by Dylan storming off."

"Wait? Dylan is still worked up about Talen?" Gabe seemed genuinely surprised as he exchanged a glance with Ryan.

"That's what Maya said. What's the deal with that guy anyway? I've never seen Dylan like this before."

"Ancient history," Gabe said in a flat tone, then looked back toward Maya.

I could tell this Talen guy rubbed them all the wrong way, so I left it alone. Not wanting to piss Gabe off too. "Seriously, Evan needs to back off. Maya has had way too much to drink, and he is clearly taking advantage of that," Gabe seethed.

The boys have always been protective of us. Sometimes they could be a little overbearing, but at times like this I was always glad they were. Heaven help any guy that got out of line with one of us. They would have three people to answer to.

"Yeah, he sort of moved in as soon as the two of them started talking."

"He's harmless," Jake chimed in. "Don't get me wrong. He loves the ladies, but Evan would never take advantage of a girl who's had too much to drink."

"Evan or no Evan, I'm about to go protect her from herself," I stated.

"Nah, I've got her tonight. You two go enjoy yourselves. Me and Ryan will take care of Maya," Gabe said.

"Are you sure? She's going to be a handful."

"I'm sure. Besides, you'll have her all night," Gabe teased. "Now go and try to have some fun tonight."

I let out a small laugh because it was true. If she kept this up I would most certainly have to take care of her all night. "Thanks, Gabe."

"You're welcome. Now go before I change my mind."

With that we were off. That was the most Gabe and I had talked all week, and I wasn't quite ready to walk away now that he was finally talking to me. Not that he wouldn't talk to me when we ran into each other, it just felt off. Like he was trying to avoid me by saying the minimal amount of words possible before making an excuse to leave. But I was glad that I was going to get to spend some drama free time with Jake.

"Can Evan really be trusted?" I asked Jake as we were walking away from the group.

"I know he doesn't seem like it, but the guy is all talk. Get him out of a group and he's actually a nice guy."

"Really?" I asked in disbelief.

Jake stopped and faced me, placing both hands on my shoulders. "Really," he said reassuring me.

"OK."

"OK?" Jake questioned, as if to double check I meant what I was saying.

"Yes, OK," I smiled.

I couldn't keep from thinking that I had the sweetest boyfriend ever. I knew that if Jake thought I was at all truly worried about Maya and Evan, we would have walked right back over there and spent the rest of our night watching over those two. I trusted Jake, and if Jake said Evan was harmless, then Evan was harmless.

When Jake was satisfied that I meant what I was saying, he grabbed my hand and led me over to where some people were hanging out around a bonfire. We found an empty chair and Jake sat down, pulling me down to him. I settled in his arms, and we sat there watching the fire for a while – not saying anything and not needing to. We were both content with watching the flames and simply being close to one another.

"I'm really happy you came out with me tonight," Jake said, breaking the silence and running the back of his fingers down the side of my arm.

Goose bumps erupted where his fingers had touched, and I caught my breath as I turned to face him. "Of course. Why would I not have?"

"I don't know," he shrugged still staring at the flames, "Maybe you'd want to hang out with your friends or have a girls night or something."

"Well, now I get to see my friends and my cute new boyfriend too."

"He sounds like a cool guy," Jake said, now smiling and looking at me.

"Well, he thinks so," I teased.

I barely got my last sentence out before Jake grabbed my face and gently connected his lips to mine. I don't know how he did it, but every time he kissed me my body responded in a way I wasn't used to. Jake must have sensed it because he deepened the kiss, wrapping his arms around me and holding me tight, sending off about a million different sensations from where his fingertips gripped my back. Both of us were breathing heavy when he broke the kiss.

"I have to stop, Emma," he growled in a tone that caused my body to betray me and lean back into him before

I even realized what I was doing. "I'm sorry I can't," he said in a more even tone, stopping me by grabbing both of my shoulders.

"What's wrong?" I half whined when I spoke next, causing myself to blush. *Stupid betraying body. I have got to get myself in check around this guy.* I paused for a moment until I could trust myself to speak. "Did I do something wrong?"

Jake looked at me with a look that I couldn't tell was concern or frustration. "Hell, no. You're doing everything right. That's the problem. If I don't stop now, I would have a really hard time stopping myself from picking you up out of this chair and carrying you back over to my truck."

"Oh," was all I could get out, as I felt the heat in my face rise once I realized why he had to stop.

"Emma," Jake began while grabbing my face and making me look at him, switching to the voice he uses whenever he is serious about something. "I'll never take things farther than you want me to. And I have a feeling me carrying you back over to my truck isn't something you're ready for."

I just shook my head, not trusting myself to speak. I couldn't trust what I would say or do around this boy. Heck, I just made out with him in the middle of a party. Even though I don't think anyone noticed because most people are either too drunk to care or are doing the same thing. Still, it is not something I would normally do.

"That's what I thought," he said sweetly, still using his serious tone. "I really do care about you, Emma."

"I know."

"Want to go walk around or just get out of this chair?"

"Yes," I laughed. "Getting out of this chair would be good."

We attempted to stand up, but somehow our feet got tangled or we tripped over the chair or something because just as soon as I was up, I was going back down and Jake was going with me. I landed with a thud right on my back. When I looked up at Jake he was holding himself up right above me. Our eyes met and we both froze.

"OK, we definitely have to get out of this area." Jake quickly stood up then helped me up.

"Agreed," I replied while brushing the dirt off the back of me.

We were walking away from the bonfire when we ran into Gabe and Ryan.

"Hey, have you guys seen Maya? I turned around for like a second to get another beer, and when I looked up her and Evan were gone." Gabe spoke with disdain looking directly at Jake, slowly enunciating Evan's name, not bothering to hide his agitation.

"No. Sorry man, we haven't," Jake lilted, still clearly amused from our little spill.

"You think this is funny, Reynolds?" Ryan jumped in. "We can't find our very drunk friend who happened to disappear with one of your friends."

"Whoa. Everybody chill out." I stepped in between them with my arms out as if that would somehow diffuse all the rising testosterone. "Nobody thinks this is funny. And before you freak out, you have to think about Maya. It's not like Evan had to drag her away to a dark corner. This is Maya we are talking about."

Before I could say anything else, we heard a voice that sounded like Maya...screaming something. We all looked at each other, then took off in the direction of the yelling. At first I was relieved to find Maya standing fully clothed in the entrance of the barn with Evan a few steps behind her. Then I turned to see a not-so-dressed Dylan with some girl I didn't know covering herself up the best she could.

"What the hell. Is. This?" Maya shouted a second and a third time.

"Don't act so innocent," Dylan spat, still scrambling to get dressed. "It's not like you weren't coming in here with him to do the exact same thing."

Evan threw his arms in the air. "Look man, don't get the wrong idea..."

"You're right," Maya shouted angrily with tears building in her eyes. "I was bringing a guy in here who actually knew what he was doing." Then she kissed a very shocked Evan.

"Figures. Slut," Dylan shot back as he walked out of the barn.

As soon as Dylan and the little tramp he brought in here were both out of sight, Maya crumbled to the floor and broke into tears. Ryan and Gabe were clearly pissed. Before I could say anything, Gabe was asking Maya what

99

happened – never taking his eyes off of Evan. I hadn't even realized Jake had grabbed my hand until I felt him tense up, getting ready to help his friend if Ryan and Gabe started something.

Through her sobs Maya told the boys to leave Evan alone. She said that she had started not to feel well and he was kind enough to ask her if she wanted to go somewhere quieter and where she didn't have to worry about puking in front of everyone. Evan took that time to defend himself.

"Seriously guys. She just wanted to get away from everyone. I was just trying to help," he said nervously and then looked at Jake, "Tell them man. I would never take advantage of a girl."

All eyes were on Jake. "I already told them you were a big softy who was all talk." Jake's words caused Ryan and Gabe to both relax a little bit.

"Shit, Jake. I said help. Not ruin my reputation."

The guys were looking back at Maya who was now crying into my shoulder.

"Maya, honey. Can you finish calling off the dogs so they don't beat Evan's face in?" I asked.

She pulled it together the best she could, then turned and looked at them with puffy eyes. "Both of you settle the hell down. If either of you hurt a hair on his head you'll have me to answer to. Now, if you insist on beating the shit out of anyone, why don't you focus on Dylan who brought me here, ditched me, and then hooked up with some whore. Mmmkay?"

She finished with as much attitude as she could manage before returning to cry on my shoulder. Gabe and Ryan both apologized for almost jumping Evan and then thanked him for looking out for Maya. Evan, now relieved, told them not to worry about it and that he would have done the same thing for one of his friends.

Jake suggested we take Maya back to my house, and I gave him a grateful smile. I know this is not how either of us wanted the night to end, so I made a mental note to make it up to him later.

Once Ryan and Gabe knew we would be taking care of Maya, they both looked at each other and then said they had to go. I knew they were going to find Dylan and, quite frankly, Dylan deserved whatever they dished out.

Jake and I walked Maya out to his truck. Jake helped me set Maya up in the backseat with a bottle of water and a trash bag just in case she got sick. We rode pretty quietly back to my house. When we got out, Maya insisted that she could make it in without the trash bag, and in true Maya fashion suddenly looked as happy and sober as ever. I told Jake I was going to make sure she got in OK then would run back out.

When we walked inside, my dad looked up from the book he was reading in his favorite chair. "Should I be concerned that you two are home forty-five minutes before curfew?" he asked amused.

"Mr. C, is it really so strange that we value our sleep more than our social life?" Maya joked back like everything was totally normal.

My dad chuckled and said from that moving speech he was going to turn in early as well. The two of them high-fived and I just rolled my eyes. We all said goodnight, and my dad headed to my parents' room while we went upstairs.

As soon as we walked into my room, Maya crumbled again. She really had gotten good at acting like everything was OK in front of people – scary good actually. How she could go from drunken tears to totally fine I will never know. Guess she has her jerk of a father to thank for that. If she ever shows she's upset in front of him, it just makes it worse.

I got some pajamas out while Maya washed her face. When she walked out of my bathroom, I handed them over to her.

"Hey, will you be OK if I run back out and say goodnight to Jake?"

"You know me. I'll be fine."

"I do know you. That's why I'm asking."

"Whatever, biatch. Go say goodnight to your man."

"Love ya, skank. I'll be right back."

"Hussy," she called out as I walked out of my room.

I smiled to myself as I crept down my stairs. The day she looses that "Mayaness" is the day I'll be really worried about her. Until that happens, I know she'll always be alright.

I opened my front door as quietly as I could and made my way over to Jake's truck.

"Maya OK?" He asked.

"She will be."

"You didn't run into your parents did you?"

"Yup. She even talked to my dad."

"You're kidding."

"Nope," I said popping the P. "It's amazing how that girl can pull it together in a snap."

"I would have liked to have seen that," Jake looked amused.

"Hang around long enough and you'll definitely get to see Maya's famous pull it all together act."

"I'm planning on it." Jake pulled me closer to him and rested his hands on my waist.

"I was kinda hoping that you would say that."

"Come to think of it, I'm starting to plan on a lot of things with you," he said with a handsome smirk.

"Oh yeah? Like what?" I asked while absentmindedly brushing some of his tousled hair out of his eyes. His hands tensed at my touch, and I had to admit that I liked that I got to him too.

He cleared his throat, "Well. I would like to take you to the movies."

"And?" I playfully demanded, while sweeping my hand through his hair, purposefully trying to get another reaction.

"And?" he questioned as a small smile tugged at the corners of his mouth. I bit my lower lip to fight back a smile as I nodded my head. "And I still need to teach you how to shoot." His eyes were on my lips as he pulled me closer, gripping the back of my shirt.

"And?"

"And take you to get ice cream again because you're adorable when you can't decide what flavor to get," he said in a hoarse whisper.

"And?" I managed in a heavy breath as he connected his lips to mine.

"And this," he replied against my mouth.

His hands gripped the small of my back. As he deepened the kiss, he ran one hand up and gripped the back of my neck causing a moan to escape my lips.

"Emma," Jake growled. Just like earlier, he began to pull away. But something about being out here, with only him, under the stars, I wasn't ready to stop. I leaned back into him and kissed him again. He briefly hesitated before scooting back in his truck and lifting me up with him. He secured one of my legs on either side of him and kissed me like he needed me to breathe.

Chapter Seven

The next morning Maya was already awake when I woke up. She was sitting up eating cereal and watching the weekend installment of the Today Show.

"Morning, Maya," I said groggily, sitting up.

"Finally, Em! I have been waiting for your ass to wake up. I was about to have to do something drastic to wake you," she teased.

I glanced over at my alarm clock. "Maya, you do realize it's only nine thirty."

"Yeah. Think about how much of the day has already been wasted."

"Help! My best friend is a freak!" I said loudly.

Not long after my outburst, my sister came flying into my room.

"Glad you're awake. I have a plan," McKenzie beamed.

Maya and I just looked at each other.

"Great. You have a plan. Now what are we talking about?" I asked as Maya took another bite of her cereal.

"To get Ryan to realize I'm not just some little kid anymore," she said like it was obvious.

"Right. And how are you going to do that?"

"This should be good," Maya uttered as milk dripped down her chin.

"Please don't get milk, especially after it has been in your mouth, in my bed."

Maya looked at me and wiped her chin with the corner of her sleeve, then smiled at me with cereal in her teeth.

"You're disgusting."

"Hello? Anyone care to hear my plan?" my sister whined.

"Oh yeah. Plan. Ryan. Go."

"OK, so you know how I've been trying like extra hard to get Ryan to notice me lately?"

"Um, yeah," I said, making it sound more like a question.

"Great. Well my plan is to do exactly the opposite."

"You've lost me, Kenz."

"OK. So instead of going out of my way to try to get him to notice me, I'm just going to stop." She carried on like it was the most obvious answer in the world. "I'm not going to look or talk to him anymore than I would anyone else. I'm even going to date someone in my grade. Genius, right?"

"So, how exactly is this going to work?"

"Reverse psychology, silly," again saying it like it was the most obvious answer in the world.

"Great. Well, you can try your theory in a couple hours," Maya chimed in, cueing both Kenzie and I to look at her. "What? I thought we could use some hang out time with our friends. And that will give you a chance to talk to Gabe sans Jake."

"What about Dylan?" I asked in a knowing tone.

"What Dylan Andrews decides to do in his free time is his business. He made that perfectly clear last night."

"Alright. Well, on that note I'm going to go back to my room," Kenzie let out.

I continued to look at Maya. As soon as my sister had closed my door behind her I began. "Maya, are you sure this is a good idea?"

"Yes, it's fine, I thought we had something. We clearly don't. So we are friends."

"Just like that? Are you sure? I mean, last night..."

"Yes, Em. It's fine," she said sharply. "I should have known better. This is Dylan. He is who he is."

"And you are you. The two of you are like a match made in..."

"Don't, Em. OK? Just don't," she pleaded.

I knew she wasn't really OK with this, but this is what Maya does best: suppress, deny, and act like everything is fine.

"OK," I said with a smile, squeezing her hand. "Lunch with the boys it is."

* * *

I have to admit, I was a little nervous about how lunch was going to go down. Dylan was awkward at first but a few looks from Ryan and Gabe and everything seemed to be fine. It also helped that Maya acted totally fine, being her usual self and interacting with the guys like always. I had to hand it to her. If I would have caught the guy I was head over heals for sleeping with some random girl whenever I thought we were finally going to get together, there is no way I would be fine with hanging out, much less acting chummy, the next day.

My mom was none the wiser. She was just happy she had a reason to cook for everyone. When I told her the guys were coming over for lunch, I didn't even have to ask her if she would make something. She quickly asked me if pulled pork sandwiches were OK. Mom had always loved to cook and jumped at any reason that allowed her to.

"Smells awesome, Mrs. C.," Dylan practically cooed. He walked over and stood next to the pot of shredded pork that my mother was seasoning and took a big whiff.

"Well then, just wait until you taste it!" mom exclaimed, while swatting Dylan's hand away as he was trying to sneak a bite.

"Can't wait. You know I love your cooking, Mrs. C." My mom turned to put the spices back in the cabinet as Dylan reached over and quickly snatched some pulled pork between his fingers and popped it in his mouth. "You were right. So good," he muttered with his mouth full.

108

My mom looked at Dylan and shook her head with an amused grin on her face. "Don't make me call your mother, mister. Or better yet, I'm going to let everyone else make a plate first," she teased, while shooing him away from the stovetop.

Dylan faked a concerned expression. "Come on, Mrs. C. You wouldn't punish a man for not being able to resist your cooking now would you?" he finished with big puppy dog eyes.

Yep. Dylan was clearly no longer bothered by last night's events and was back to acting like his typical suck-up self. This is where I would normally jump in and make some wisecrack remark about him buttering up my mom, but last night had affected me more than I thought. I could not think of a single thing to say that was not laced with something that would let on how pissed I was at him. Plus, I really didn't want my mom to pick up on something and me have to try to explain what happened last night. I don't know how Maya does it.

"You're awfully quiet over there, Em," Dylan started with that typical smirk. I guess I wasn't the only one that noticed my missing witty remark.

"I suppose I'm just hungry," I said with a forced smile. "I didn't eat breakfast because by the time I woke up, I knew I would be eating pulled pork sandwiches in just a few hours, and I love pulled pork sandwiches. And I knew they. Were worth. Waiting for."

Sensing my frustration, Gabe walked over and put his hand on my shoulder. He must have shot Dylan a look because Dylan made a "what" face before walking over to sit at the table.

"I suppose," Maya began, dragging out the end of her word, "that we should feed Emma then." She was looking directly at me, and I knew for her sake I was going to have to try harder to get through this delightfully awkward lunch.

"Alrightie then. Everyone come make a plate." Mom was holding up two plates. "I'm going to take this back to your father and keep him company while he works. Kenzie," she yelled up the stairs as she walked by. "Better come make you a plate before these boys eat it all."

My sister came bee bopping down the stairs. "Hey, Em, do you mind if I hop in front of the line? I was going to make a quick plate then go finish getting ready. Mom is going to take me to meet some. Friends. For ice cream here pretty quick," she said in a singsong voice, emphasizing the word friends.

"Sounds like little Kenzie has a date," Gabe teased.

"Oh hush, Gabe. There are going to be a few people there. It's not like it's going to be just me and Logan." McKenzie broke out into a huge smile as Gabe gestured for her to go to the front of the line. Kenzie quickly made a plate then started to leave the kitchen. As she walked by me, she stopped. "Oh, hey, Em. Do you mind if I borrow that blue top you wore on your date with Jake last weekend?"

Maya leaned in and whispered, "Oh, she's good," causing me to let out a small laugh.

110

"Nope," I said amused. "Go right ahead."

"Eeek!" she squealed. "You're the best!" Her eyes shot a quick glance over at Ryan that I would have missed if I hadn't been watching her intently, and a smile tugged at the corners of her mouth as she met my gaze again.

After that little performance, even I would have really believed Kenzie was into Logan if I wouldn't have known about her plan. I just can't believe she's going through all this trouble to make a guy, whose not even interested, jealous.

"Nice choice, Kenz," Maya chimed in. "That shirt really hugs in all the right places." She said, winking at Kenzie. Then gave her a high-five.

"Wait? Logan Rivers? Isn't that guy a freshman?" Ryan asked slightly annoyed, causing Maya and I to exchange glances.

"Yep. Just like me. And he is so hot. I can't believe he is finally interested in me!"

"Whatever. Have fun with your boy crush," Ryan scoffed. This time clearly annoyed, causing Maya and I to exchange glances again.

"Thanks!" was the last thing Kenzie said before running back upstairs with her plate of food."

"You alright there, buddy?" I asked Ryan.

"Yeah. I just think she's a little young to be dating."

"Okie dokie. I'll be sure to pass that on to my parents. Thanks for looking out for her. I think?" I was partly amused and partly confused about what just happened. After that little incident, I couldn't help but wonder if maybe Jake was right – that Ryan might actually have a thing for Kenzie. Nah, it couldn't be. He had to just be looking out for her. Right?

The rest of lunch went by like nothing had changed. Even Gabe and I were talking like we used to. It seemed like forever since just the five of us hung out like this, and I had to admit it was nice.

"Be right back. I have to pee," I announced as I stood up.

"Thanks for letting us know," Ryan joked.

"No prob."

I went up to my room to use the bathroom, and on my way out I heard voices that caused me to stop before exiting my room.

"Maya, will you please stop? We need to talk," Dylan pleaded in a hushed voice.

"No, we don't. And, Dylan, I really have to go to the bathroom," She replied like nothing was wrong.

"Maya, will you please talk to me?" This time there was an urgency in his voice.

"Who you choose to do in your free time is up to you," she let out like it was nothing.

"I screwed up big. I was drunk. She didn't mean anything to me. You acting like nothing is wrong is killing me," he said defeated.

"Is killing you?" Maya uttered in a tone that made it apparent that Dylan had finally gotten to her. "Oh I'm sorry, it must have been so hard on you for me to walk in and

112

catch you having sex with some slut who dropped her panties for the first drunk guy she met."

"Maya, how can I make you see how sorry I am? I mean look at me...you know me," Dylan said, begging for her forgiveness.

"You're right. I do know you. I know that it only takes one look from a girl to get you to take her into another room. And to think, I really thought you were capable of a relationship. Well Dylan, I guess the joke's on me."

With that, Maya walked into my room with tears in her eyes, stopping briefly when she saw me. I mouthed, "I'm sorry." She shook her head and continued into my bathroom.

Before walking out of my room I heard Dylan's voice again, which caused me to stop, again. "I screwed up man. I fucking screwed up."

"I told you that last night," Gabe replied. "What's done is done. You have to let it play out however it's going to play out."

"Not if I can help it. It made me crazy to see her flirting with that Evan guy, especially after everything that Talen prick said. I thought. Well it doesn't matter what I thought. I love her Gabe. It took me banging some chick, then seeing the hurt in her eyes when she saw me to realize it, but I love her. I never want to hurt her like that again, and I will make this right." Dylan sounded so choked up it was hard not to feel a little sorry for him.

Gabe paused for a moment before he responded, "I know you do, man."

113

Dylan sniffed, then said he had to go. Gabe told him he'd let everyone know he left. Dylan thanked him, and then I heard him head down the stairs. I was so glad Maya didn't hear any of this. This was definitely something she would want to know later, but right now it would just make things worse. She also needed to hear it from him. I knew it would just make her more angry if I told her. She would say something like, "That dick head didn't even have the balls to tell me himself."

Once I no longer heard steps going downstairs, I gave it one more second and then finally left my room myself almost bumping into Gabe.

"Ope, sorry," we both laughed.

"Did you hear any of that?" Gabe asked.

"The whole thing. Including when it was he and Maya. I was just trying to pee but ended up getting stuck in my room so I didn't walk into the complete mess that is currently Maya and Dylan."

"I know she's your best friend, but don't say anything to her, alright?"

"I won't. That is all something he needs to tell her himself. And it is not something she needs to hear the day after he hooked up with someone else. It makes it feel tainted." I gave a halfhearted smile before turning to head down stairs.

Gabe stopped me, "I wouldn't go down there if I were you."

"What? Why?"

"Kenzie walked down shortly after Dylan went to find Maya. She and Ryan got into it. That's why I came up here in the first place. I left one argument to find another one."

"What the heck is wrong with him today? Did you think it was weird that he acted strange about Logan?"

"I mean a little. But Ryan has always been protective of Kenzie. I guess we all have. I did find it odd that he is the one that picked the fight with her when she came back downstairs, though."

"Good Lord," I said letting out a breath. "Maybe Jake is right after all."

"About Jake," he started, clearing his throat, "I know I haven't really been around this last week."

"Yeah, I noticed that. I've missed you, Gabe."

"I know. I'm sorry. It has just been hard seeing you with him. You know? At first I thought it would make it easier on all of us if I just backed off, but then I lose you completely. I don't want to lose you completely, Em." He paused for a second to put a loose piece of hair behind my ear. "I want you to know that I will always be here, even if right now you just need me as a friend. But hear me when I say, I will never give up on you."

"Gabe," I croaked out – not realizing how much his speech had affected me until I tried to speak.

Without hesitation, after hearing my voice crack, Gabe scooped me up in his arms and held me. He didn't loosen his grip until I pulled back.

I took a breath, "Gabe. You know I love you, but as a friend. I really do care about Jake."

115

"I know you do right now. But like I said, I'm not going anywhere." After he finished talking he turned and walked downstairs, leaving me at the top, standing there speechless.

After a few moments, I heard someone behind me. I turned to find Maya waving a pair of my white panties in the air. "Is it safe to come out?" she giggled.

"Oh my God!" I gasped, looking back downstairs to make sure no one was standing there. Then I walked into my room, forcing a laughing Maya to go backwards.

"It's my version of a white flag. I didn't want to walk out of here empty handed."

"Good Lord," I said snatching my panties out of her hand and closing them back up in my drawer. When I turned around she was standing there looking at me, her smile now gone.

"I guess we both got stuck in here today, didn't we?"

"I guess we did. Listen, Maya. I'm so sorry about Dylan. He can be a real jerk."

"Humph. It sounds like you're defending him."

"Heck no." I thought about saying that there is always more to the story. That this is Dylan we were talking about. The fact that he tried to apologize at all was huge, much less that he was all choked up about it and practically begging for her forgiveness. But I knew Maya, and I knew that right now none of that mattered. Her hurt was too fresh. So I left it at that.

"Anyway, what just happened with Gabe?"

116

"I don't know. He like avoided me all week, then jumped me with that." I was still trying to wrap my own mind around it.

Maya looked at me with that mischievous grin of hers, "I told you that boy was in love with you."

"Great. Now I have to worry about you too?" I joked.

"Come on, biatch. Let's go back downstairs. I need to get away from this room before something else happens."

"I hear that. Right behind you."

I followed Maya downstairs over to where the boys were sitting on the couch watching ESPN. As I walked by, Gabe snatched me and pulled me down to his lap. I looked up to see Maya staring at me. "I'm just saying," she mumbled.

I scooted off Gabe and he leaned over, "What's that about?"

"Nothing," I darted my eyes toward Maya.

Once the boys left, Maya and I put on a movie. We had just put the popcorn in a bowl and were bringing it into the living room when my phone beeped.

"Jake or Gabe?" she asked putting a handful of popcorn in her mouth.

"Funny," I said taking my phone out of my back pocket. I glanced at my text message and could not contain the smile that broke out on my face.

"Jake," she stated.

"That obvious?"

"From the look on your face, yes. Now, hussy, are you going to tell me what he said or what?"

117

"He wants to know if I'm free tonight."

"Say yes," she said, like duh.

"I'm not just going to leave you, especially after the whole Dylan thing last night and then again today."

"Well if you don't, then I'm going to be pissed at you too. At least one of us should be able to get some tonight."

I looked at her with wide eyes, "Oh my God, Maya."

She looked at me with her little smirk. "Well, you can't say that you haven't at least thought about it. Oh, don't look at me like that. From the way you described how that boy kisses you, I know you've thought about it."

"OK! But it's not going to happen tonight."

"I knew it! Now text that boy yes or I'll do it for you."

Knowing that there was no arguing with Maya at this point, I picked up my phone and texted Jake. I explained why I couldn't leave Maya tonight but that he could join us as long as he didn't mind sweat pants and a chick flick. After a few seconds he responded, saying he understood and that he in no way minded sweat pants. We finalized plans and then I set my phone beside me so I could focus on the movie.

Maya cleared her throat causing me to look over at her. "Well?" she asked impatiently.

I shoved another handful of popcorn in my mouth not bothering to finish chewing before I responded, "I told Jake I couldn't leave my bestie in her hour of need."

"My God, Emma. I'm not dying," she complained, completely unfazed by the popcorn hanging out of my mouth.

"Let me finish," I said mischievously, causing Maya to get quiet and look at me questionably. "I also said that he could join us if he didn't mind sweat pants and countless hours of sappy movies with Gerard Butler and Matthew McConaughey."

"Well?" she gestured with her hand.

I put another handful of popcorn in my mouth. "Well, he asked what type of sweat pants. When I specified yoga pants, he said he would be right over," I somehow managed without breaking a smile, although the same couldn't be said for Maya.

"I knew I liked that boy. Now let's go put on some yoga pants. By the way, you're disgusting." Then she took a mouthful of popcorn herself and smiled.

It took longer than I expected for Jake to arrive. When the doorbell finally rang, I ran downstairs to meet my boyfriend. I opened the door to see Jake standing there with two gallons of ice cream – one in each hand.

"Girls eat ice cream when they are pissed at boys, right?"

"You sir, are too much. I mean, is there anything wrong with you or am I really dating the world's perfect boyfriend?" I teased.

Jake looked at me with that impossible smile of his and had just stepped in to kiss me when Maya piped up. I could practically hear her rolling her eyes. "You two are annoyingly adorable. Wait. Is that ice cream?" She asked as she grabbed both gallons from Jake and took them into the kitchen with us in tow.

119

Maya wasted no time digging into the two containers. I looked over to witness her interchanging a scoop into her mouth, then into a bowl. Jake and I watched as she continued this until her bowl was full of both types of ice cream.

"And you said I was disgusting?" I teased.

Jake looked from me to Maya, then stated, "I'm not even going to ask. Anyway, I was just going to drop these off real quick then head out to meet up with Evan."

I couldn't help the look of disappointment that took over my face when Jake said he wasn't staying. Jake noticed too and started to say something.

"Liar!" Maya exclaimed causing us both to look at her. "It was all about the pants. Yoga pants."

"Well, can you blame a man?" he shot back, pretending to be offended.

"With an ass like hers, no I can't," she said before grabbing her bowl and a container of ice cream and then carrying them into the living room. "Oh, and Jakie Pooh. Tell Evan hi for me, will ya?"

"Yeah, sure Maya," he said loud enough for her to hear him in the other room.

"Maya, I'll be right back. Gunna walk Jake out then we can restart the movie," I called out.

"Mmkay. Take your time!" she shouted with a mouthful of ice cream.

Outside Jake started his truck and turned down the radio, then took me in his arms.

"I thought you were going to stay," I pouted.

"Don't get me wrong. I want to stay, especially when you are in those pants. But I have this feeling that tonight your friend needs you without your "annoyingly adorable" boyfriend doting all over you," he said, mocking Maya's tone.

"Yeah, yeah," I allowed myself to collapse into his chest. "That doesn't mean I don't want you here doting all over me. But thanks."

He lifted my chin so that our eyes met. "Anytime, darlin'," he uttered in a low, sexy drawl.

"Are you using Evan's line so that I will kiss you?"

"Well I don't know. Is it working?" he asked as he leaned down and connected his lips to mine.

Chapter Eight

During the next several weeks I couldn't keep from noticing that Maya and Evan seemed to always find each other; and I clearly wasn't the only one. Dylan and Maya hadn't said a word to each other since that Saturday at my house. But, every time Dylan saw Maya and Evan together, Dylan looked like he was about to kill Evan. When I asked Maya about it, she was quick to say that she and Evan were just friends and that Dylan Andrews was not allowed to care who her friends were. I didn't bring it up again.

Keeping on the avoiding trend, after Ryan got over his pissy stage he started avoiding my sister like the plague. It was to the point that he wouldn't even come to the house if Kenzie was going to be there. By how strangely he had been acting, I was really starting to suspect that Jake was right about him being into McKenzie. He certainly wasn't avoiding her because she was being annoying. In fact, she started treating Ryan like all the other guys after she started dating Logan.

Gabe and I seemed to be back to normal. I was glad about that because I wasn't sure how things were going to be after his heartfelt confession. I had to admit that it was nice to be able to hang out with Gabe and go to lunch and stuff like we used too without it being awkward. He even started sneaking through my window again occasionally. Jake wasn't too thrilled about that, but I assured him he had nothing to worry about.

One night when Gabe had crawled through my window, I asked him if he knew anything about the Maya and Dylan situation. He said Dylan wouldn't talk about it any more than Maya. That all Dylan would say is "I will fix this."

"This is his idea of fixing it?" I asked in disbelief. "I mean they won't say a word to each other, much less be in the same general space as the other one."

"I know. It doesn't make any sense to me either."

"Well, I for one am tired of feeling like I have to choose sides. I miss being able to all hang out like we used to."

Gabe squished himself next to me in my bowl chair, "Me too, Em. But it is not just those two that make it hard for us all to hang out like we used to."

"Yeah. I know. And I've about had it up to here with this little attitude Ryan has developed as well. I have the right mind to sit all three of them down and not let them get up until they can just move past everything and let us be friends again."

"If only it were that simple."

"I know. But it gets messy when feelings are involved."

"Yeah, and all three..." he stopped midsentence.

"Well, anyway..."

"Wait. What did you just say?" I questioned as he started to say something else.

"Nothing. I was trying to say it's late so I better get going, but you cut me off."

"Uh, no. You said three. What did you mean by three?"

"It's late. I'm tired. I misspoke," he countered, starting to get up.

"Gabriel Shawn Walters. Sit yourself back down," I said in a tone that made him stop and sink back into the bowl chair. I waited till he looked at me. "You said three. Now you tell me the truth. You were referring to Ryan as the third. Does it have anything to do with him having feelings for McKenzie?"

He took a moment to just stare back at me. "Em, don't worry yourself about this. Nothing happened or will happen."

"What do you mean by nothing happened?"

Gabe leaned forward and put his head between his hands, running his fingers through his hair. "Oh God. He is going to be so pissed if he ever finds out I told you. That is if he even remembers saying anything to me."

"Told me what, Gabe?"

He turned to look at me, dropping one of his hands so that I could see his face. "Listen, Em. Before I say anything, you have to know that nothing happened and that nothing will ever happen. You know Ryan, and you know the type of guy that he is."

"OK," I said slowly.

"I mean it, Em. You have always been really protective of Kenz. And you should be, cause she is your little sister. But in this case, you also have to know who your friend is and not jump to conclusions."

"OK," I said again.

"OK." He slowly sat up. "So something happened over the summer. Shit, I mean something didn't happen. Well it did, but in his head. Damn, this is not coming out right. Just let me start over."

"By all means..."

"Alright. So you know how Ryan has basically been acting weird since Kenzie has been back from camp this summer."

"Yeah. And?"

"Well. It may have something to do with the fact that he doesn't view her as a little kid anymore," he said with a winced expression.

"What?"

"Em, nothing has happened."

"Yeah, you mentioned that. But have I mentioned she's fifteen?"

"Valid point. But, Em, even you admit she does not look fifteen."

"Are you defending him?" I asked in a tone torn between anger and understanding.

"I don't have to defend him. He hasn't done anything wrong. He can't help that your sister has gone from a little girl to sexy as hell in one summer."

"Uh," I gawked, "She's fifteen."

"Yes, we've been over this. We also both know that she looks older than you, acts your age, and that because she's fifteen Ryan would never do anything. She's always been closer to him than with Dylan or me. When you think about it, it makes since that they would eventually see each other as more than friends."

"But she's fifteen," I muttered.

Gabe let out a breath. "Oh my God. You're relentless. Can you honestly say you didn't see this coming?"

I took a moment to think about everything before I responded. "No," I finally said, "I can't say that I didn't see this coming. She has really liked him since the first time she met him, but it was always a silly crush because he was so much older. And you're right. If you didn't know her, you would never guess she was so young. She doesn't act her age and she certainly doesn't look it. But if he ever. Tries. Anything. Before she's eighteen, you better kill him or I will."

Gabe let out a relieved laugh. "Deal." He reached up to rub his eyes, then turned to look back at me. "But, Em, you know he never would. And it's been killing him – trying to fight any feelings for her. It didn't help when she was throwing herself at him. Then, knowing he can't have her, he has to watch her date another guy. Imagine how hard that is for him, especially knowing that little hornball has one thing on his mind."

"Please, Logan is a nice guy."

"There is no such thing as a nice guy. Especially at fifteen. I guarantee you that guy has one thing on his mind. And it's the same thing all guys think about when it comes to the Crawford sisters."

"Eww. Too much information." And it was. I did not want to think about any guy thinking about my little sister that way. Although I have to admit, I liked to hear that some guys really found me that attractive. I mean, I'm not blind. I know I'm pretty, but Gabe makes it sound like he thinks I'm a knockout or something. And if that's the case, he really is blind.

"Yeah, now think about how Ryan feels. Knowing she is with a guy that doesn't care about her the way he would or who would take care of her the way that any of us would. At least you know Ryan would respect her."

"Yeah. I guess." I took in a breath looking around the room before staring back at Gabe.

"I mean damn. Ryan has been through hell trying not to feel anything for her. Can you imagine what it would be like to suddenly be attracted to someone that you have viewed up to this point as a little kid? Then, knowing that they were too young for you and not being able to act on it. Like that sucks."

I laughed for the first time since Gabe started talking. "You know when you put it that way, the whole thing really does suck."

"And, Em, don't let him know you know. The only reason I know is because of quite a few beers and a few other reasons. He probably doesn't even remember saying anything to me. And I swear to you, if he ever decides to act on this before she's eighteen, you can take a turn at him after Dylan and I do," he finished with that boyish grin of his.

"I'm not going to say anything. I feel like that would just make this whole thing weirder. And about the other thing, thanks."

"Any time," he said, starting to get up, "Now I really do need to get going or neither one of us is going to be able to get up tomorrow."

"You're right. And tomorrow is only Wednesday," I groaned as we walked over to my window.

Gabe turned to look back at me before he climbed out the window. "Night, Emmie," he whispered reaching out to touch my face.

"Night, Gabe," I smiled back. But there was that guilt again. I would have never thought twice about Gabe touching the side of my face before Jake; but now, knowing that for Gabe it was not just a simple touch, it had everything in my head all confused. I hate that this line got blurred and desperately wished Gabe and I could go back to

128

when we both felt like we were just friends. I can't put my finger on it, but in a way I feel like I'm starting to lose my friend.

Needless to say, I walked groggily into school the following morning. I saw Dylan first, standing with a group of guys from the tennis team. Come to think of it, over the last several weeks I've only seen Dylan hanging out with guys. And he certainly did not have his usual girl or two hanging all over him. I couldn't help but wonder why I was just picking up on that. But I was quickly distracted from that when I finally spotted Maya, who was standing with Evan and Jake.

I made my way over to them just in time to hear Evan and Maya say something that I didn't understand, then both start laughing. I looked over at Jake and he shrugged, then grabbed my hand, lacing our fingers together – clearly not understanding what they were talking about either. Maya stopped laughing when she saw me.

"Look what the cat dragged in. I mean it literally looks like someone dragged you in. Not get much sleep last night, Em?"

"No. Gabe came over last night and didn't leave till late."

I felt Jake tense. "So that explains why you never called me back last night," he was trying to sound nonchalant, even though I could obviously see how much what I had just said bothered him.

"Oh crap. Jake, I'm so sorry. We got to talking, then it got late, and I completely forgot," I gasped, feeling terrible, which seemed to lighten Jake's mood a little.

"So what were y'all talking about that required him to stay over so late?" Maya asked, taking another bite of the apple I didn't realize she had until then.

"Oh nothing," I said in a way that I hoped would satisfy them enough to move on to something else. Yet, it seemed to have the opposite effect. I felt Jake tense up again, and I could tell he was about to say something before Maya chimed in.

"Oh crap. Don't anybody look now," she panicked. "Evan, just go with it. I'll explain later," she uttered quickly, but desperately, right before she kissed him.

I was totally confused and then even more shocked when Evan wrapped his arms around her, pulled her close, and kissed her back. It's like my brain needed a moment to process what it was seeing before I could even ask what the heck was going on. As soon as I heard Dylan's voice, it all seemed to make a little more sense.

"Come on, man. You don't have to work that hard to get Maya in the sack," he sneered, unable to sound any more like a jerk then he did in that moment. His comment also ceased Maya and Evan's lip-lock and gained both of their attention. "A little bit of whiskey and that girl is an easy lay," he continued, giving Evan a cocky wink as he slapped him on the back and kept walking. He only took a few steps before he turned back to face our direction. "Oh, and Jack and coke is her poison. Works every time. Isn't that right, babe?" he finished slowly, maliciousness dripping off every word as he spoke.

Maya's eyes glazed over as he walked away and realization swept over me. She hadn't just been hurt because she found Dylan with another girl when she thought they were going to get together. She had slept with him. She had slept with Dylan, and he was the first guy Maya had sex with that she really cared about. And to make matters worse, he just announced it to everyone in the hallway. You have got to be kidding me.

"Maya..." I started, unable to hide the sadness I felt for my friend in my voice.

"No, Emma. Just stop. This time I can't take what you think you know. You, with your perfect family, perfect boyfriend, and perfect life. Just stop. I can't. I can't anymore," she shouted. She took one more breath and a tear escaped down her cheek before she turned and quickly walked away.

I'm not sure when Gabe got there or what all he heard but when I tried to go after her, he grabbed me and told me to let her go.

"She needs some time to cool off, Em," he said softly. Knowing how much it was killing me not to be able to help my best friend when she was hurting and somehow managing to be part of the problem, he added, "Just give it some time, Em, she'll come around.

Between my exhaustion from last night and everything that just happened this morning, the next thing I knew I was throwing my arms around Gabe crying silent tears. It must have surprised him because it took him a second to hug me back. He held me close until I could trust myself enough to let go without letting everyone else know that I was crying.

When I pulled back I looked around and Jake was nowhere in sight. "Where'd Jake go?"

"He walked off pretty soon after you buried yourself in my shoulder."

"Perfect! Freaking perfect!" I said louder than I meant too. "How is he ever going to believe that we are just friends when I do stuff like this? In his mind I bet he is thinking I chose you over him. Add it to the gosh darn list today."

"Em?"

"What?" I demanded, clearly frustrated.

"Why did you just choose me over him?" He asked, sounding almost afraid to ask the question.

"I...I don't know," I let out as I sunk down on the floor leaning against the lockers. "I wish we could just hit rewind and do this morning all over again." I put my hands over my face and sat there like that until the morning bell rang. Gabe was still standing there, waiting patiently, when I stood up.

"Want to just get out of here?" he offered, leaning against the lockers.

"Oh yeah, how would I explain that one to Jake? I'm just going to go to class." I threw my bag over my shoulder and turned to walk toward Spanish.

"I'm here if you need me, Em," I heard Gabe say as I walked away. I didn't stop and turn around. I just put my hand in the air and gave a little wave to let him know that I heard him.

Maya wasn't in Spanish when I got there. I couldn't find her in the halls, and when she didn't show up for the second class we had together, I knew she had left. I might as well have been gone. I spent most of my morning worrying about her. God, I just hoped she didn't do anything stupid. She never did deal well when she was this upset.

Much to my surprise, when the bell rang for lunch Jake was waiting for me by my locker. He gave me his best attempt at a smile when I walked up to him.

"Evan texted and said he took Maya home," he said in a forced voice.

"OK. Thanks. I knew she had left and was hoping she wasn't driving around by herself somewhere. She is really unpredictable when she gets like this." I starred at my locker unable to meet Jake's eyes.

He reached out, grabbed my chin, and gently turned my face toward him. He waited until our eyes met. "I'm sorry I walked off earlier, Em."

"You're sorry?" I half laughed. "I throw my arms around Gabe instead of you and you're sorry?"

"Not going to lie. I was pissed at first, but I know he's your friend and sometimes you need a friend when shit goes down," he swallowed, running his hand down my arm. "I'm here for you too, you know. I hope one day you feel like you can lean on me instead of him." I could hear the strain in his voice as he said the last part.

My eyes swelled with tears, and as soon as Jake saw them he pulled me into him. "None of that. Do you hear me? I know you could be with him if you wanted to be, but you chose me," he said, hugging me tight. "I mean you did choose me, didn't you?" he asked, pulling away and pretending to be worried.

I let out a little laugh. "I'm sorry about earlier and I'm sorry I'm an emotional mess...I'm just sorry."

Jake looked at me with that perfect smile of his while tucking away a piece of hair behind my ear. "Want to pretend that today just started?"

"More than you know."

Jake turned around and jogged a few feet away. Then he turned back around and walked toward me.

"Morning, beautiful," he said, scooping me up in a hug.

"Good morning, yourself." I played along.

A grin tugged at the corner of his mouth as he leaned down and gave me a quick peck. "Now what do you say we go get some lunch?"

"Yes, please! I'm starving."

The rest of the day went by extremely slowly. I was worried about Maya but also hurt and confused about why she had lashed out at me. She and I never fought. I was shocked when it first happened and thought it would blow over after she had some time to herself. I mean, this is me and Maya we were talking about. I didn't really expect her to stay mad. When I hadn't heard from her by the time I got to practice, I started to get irritated.

I pulled into the parking lot right behind Gabe and marched my way over to him as soon as I got out of my car.

"Like really? What is her freakin' problem? I didn't do anything."

"Good afternoon to you too there, sunshine," he replied as his passenger side door closed. I looked up to see Ryan getting out of his car.

"Yeah um, I'm just going to head to the courts and let you two work out whatever it is that y'all have going on here."

"No, it's fine Ryan. You know what's going on anyway," I spat.

"Uh, OK. I'm not sure what to do here?" Ryan said, looking a little nervous.

"Whatever." I turned back to Gabe. "I mean, I get that Dylan hurt her and that she's pissed at him. Heck, I would be too, especially knowing what I know now. But mad at me? Really?" I steamed.

Ryan relaxed a bit when he realized this was about Maya. And if I hadn't been so worked up over this issue, I probably would have probed him about why.

"Give her some space, Em. You know Maya can get a little fiery when she gets upset."

Ryan coughed, "A little fiery? You mean like a full on fireball. That's chasing you. And it's scary."

"Yeah. Just never at me."

"So that is what this is about," Gabe said, sounding amused.

I looked at him with a raised eyebrow, waiting for him to speak.

"This is y'alls first big fight."

"No. Well yes. I mean we don't really fight, especially when the other person hasn't done anything wrong." I said flustered.

"Listen, Em. You know Maya. Just give her some space right now. She'll come around."

"Yeah. Alright. But if Dylan decides to show his cocky, jerk of a self today, I'm going to peg him so hard with a tennis ball. This entire thing is his fault."

"Note to self. Do not piss Emma off at tennis practice," Ryan chimed in.

"Oh shut up. Come on, let's walk over to the courts. Jake's truck is here and he's probably wondering why I'm not up there yet."

"Heaven forbid your boy toy has to wait for you," Gabe joked.

I just rolled my eyes and then started walking with both the boys in tow.

* * *

I hit my light and crawled into bed after what felt like one of the longest days of my life. I still hadn't heard from Maya; at this point I was past mad and back to worried. This just wasn't like her. I made up my mind that I

136

was going to track that girl down tomorrow and make her talk to me if I had too.

I had just closed my eyes when I heard the tap, tap, tap on my window. When my window didn't open right away, I thought maybe just maybe Gabe decided to leave me alone and let me get some sleep after everything that happened today. I wasn't that lucky. I heard the window open and thought about throwing my pillow at him.

"Gabe. I swear to..." I started, clearly agitated, but was cut off by a voice I wasn't expecting.

"Not Gabe. Just me. But please keep going. I like you addressing Gabe when it sounds like you're going to kill him." Jake chuckled.

"Jake? What are you doing here? I mean, I'm glad you're here. I just wasn't expecting you," I rambled on while trying to smooth down any stray hairs and adjust my oversized t-shirt.

"Oh. Were you expecting someone else? I can go." I could hear the playfulness in his voice as I heard him continue toward me, causing my heart to speed up.

"No!" I said a little too quickly. I took a deep breath before answering again. "No to both, actually." I got out – more under control of my voice this time.

"Good."

Even in the dark, Jake made his way over to my bed with ease. He sat down right next to me and placed one hand on each side of me. He was close enough that I could see him looking directly at me. We sat there for a moment before either of us spoke – not that I could have if I tried.

137

Something about him being this close to me, in the dark, on my bed, with my parents right downstairs had butterflies going off in my stomach and took away my ability to trust what would come out of my mouth.

"So, what's next?" he asked as if this were the most normal thing in the world.

"Wha...what?" I asked slightly breathless. What does he mean what next? I don't even know what is going on right now.

He gave me one of those perfect smiles and had a look on his face that caused my body to react. Then suddenly he moved, pulling his hands back and standing right beside my bed. *What the heck was going on?*

"I mean, what do you and Gabe do after he crawls through your window?"

At the mention of Gabe, I felt a twinge of guilt and disappointment. Ever since I started dating Jake, a part of me has felt bad when Gabe crawled through my window. I was excited when Jake crawled through my window tonight, but now I know that he only did this so he could better understand what goes on between Gabe and I – I can't help but feel disappointed about that.

"Well, he usually waits until I'm really comfortable and almost asleep, then decides to crawl through my window. So, so far you're right on track. Then, he walks straight into my bathroom. Usually while I'm telling him how irritated I am that he is robbing me of my sleep. But knowing he won't leave until I talk to him, I storm in behind him and give him my best annoyed face."

"OK then," was all he said before turning and going into my bathroom. I let out a sigh before following him into the other room. Just like I had to do with Gabe, I turned on the light as I walked in.

"What now?" As soon as he said that, I went from disappointed to frustrated. Does he really not have enough trust in me that he felt like he had to come get a play-by-play of how things go with Gabe?

"Really? You came all the way here to reenact what it's like when Gabe crawls through my window?" I tried to not sound as frustrated as I was but clearly failed. His face turned into a frown, and he sunk down into my bowl chair.

"Can you blame me? Emma, I know he's your friend, but he is still a guy. And you...you are beautiful. And if this is what you sleep in, I really want to know what happens next," he gestured to my oversized t-shirt while now sounding frustrated himself.

"OK. Again, really? After today, did you plan on coming over here and picking a fight with me?" I was currently on the verge of being borderline mad.

Jake leaned forward and ran his fingers through his tousled hair before looking back up at me. "No. But I did want to know what it was like between the two of you. Then I see you, in this shirt that hangs just past your ass and. Damn it, Emma. Can you not see why this would be hard for me?" He sank back into the bowl chair and closed his eyes as he leaned his head back.

I wasn't stupid. Of course I knew what this had to look like from his point of view. I probably wouldn't be crazy

139

about another girl crawling through his window either. But this is just how it has always been between Gabe and I. And gah. Why did life have to get so complicated?

I walked over to Jake and reached down to grab his hand. At my touch, his eyes opened and found mine. "I know this probably looks bad and doesn't make any sense to you. I like you Jake, and if Gabe crawling through my window is going to make things wrong between us, then I'll tell him he can't do it anymore."

He made a frustrated sound as he sat up and grabbed my other hand as well. "Emma, I don't want to dictate what you can and cannot do with your friends. But I also can't sit around anymore knowing some guy is sneaking in here when you look sexy as hell." I blushed at his words and reached out to touch his face before letting my hand fall back down into his, wishing the whole time I could take away the pained expression that I know I put there.

Looking into his eyes I couldn't tell if he was mad, or hurt, or nervous, but then he took a breath, "Emma, you're not like any other girl I've dated." Nervous – he was definitely nervous. "I'm not sure what it is about you that makes me this crazy, but I know why this Gabe thing bothers me so bad." He took another deep breath and squeezed my hands a little tighter. "I love you, Emma."

All I could do was stand there with this goofy grin and look at him like an idiot while his words sank in.

"Say something please," he choked out.

"I love you too, Jake." I bit my lower lip as a huge smile spread across his face.

"Yeah?"

"Yes! Of course I do. How could I not?"

He didn't waste any time reaching up and pulling me down onto his lap so that I was straddling him. He took my face in his hands and kissed me. It started out gentle and sweet, but then his hands dropped to my bare thighs. I felt his hands tense when they made contact with my skin. He sucked in a breath, which caused a shiver to shoot down my spine. He deepened the kiss, and I felt his hands begin to creep up my leg. Instinctually, as if my hands had a mind of their own, I reached up and tangled my hands in his hair.

"Emma," Jake growled, pulling back just enough for him to speak. "If we don't stop now, I don't know if I can trust myself to stop later," he breathed heavily.

I touched my forehead to his and closed my eyes. "What if I don't want you to stop?"

As soon as my words were out, his lips found mine and his fingers ran straight up my thighs until his hands cupped over my lacey hipster panties. I was instantly glad I was wearing one of my new Pink purchases. When his fingertips tightened around my curves, I sucked in a sharp breath of air. Embarrassed, I started to pull back – stupid betraying body. I never could trust myself around this boy. But Jake didn't seem phased. He ran one of his hands up my back and pulled me back into him.

I could feel him smiling against my lips. "I love the effect I have on you, Em," he whispered, so close I could feel his breath on my neck, causing my skin to tingle on every surface his breath touched. His words managed to ease my nerves and I sank back into his kiss, losing myself until I felt his hands stop at the top of my rib cage. He must have felt my body tense because he broke the kiss, leaving us both breathing heavy. "You are calling the shots tonight, Blondie. Nothing will happen unless you want it to." he uttered huskily.

I could barely think, much less respond, as his fingers teased the top of my lacey hipsters and he peppered kisses across my collarbone. "Jake," I sighed. I could tell he enjoyed hearing his name breathlessly escaping my lips because he reconnected his lips to mine and kissed me hungrier than he had before. His hands were everywhere, roaming across my bare skin. Each pass of his fingertips made me crazy in a way I never knew was possible.

I was so lost in the moment that I almost didn't hear Jake utter, "Don't let go." When he started to move, what he said registered. Without hesitating, I wrapped my legs around his waist as he stood up from the chair. He never broke the kiss as he walked us back into my room and gently laid us back down on my bed.

Though I have never been drunk, I imagine this is what it must feel like. Your head in a blissful fog, consumed by thoughts of things you would never be brave enough to do sober. Each kiss from Jake seemed to pull me deeper and deeper into this state of being wonderfully out of control. I reached down and began to tug at Jake's shirt until it was up by his shoulders. With one smooth motion Jake lifted up and shrugged out of his soft tee, revealing his toned torso that I couldn't resist running my fingers down. I have never in my life been so bold. I knew that if there were any more light than what was being provided from the moon, my cheeks would give away what I was feeling in this moment.

Breathe, Emma, Breathe.

When I looked back up at him, he had a smug smile on his face and just like that all my hesitation went back out the window. I reached up and tangled my fingers into his hair, bringing him back down and connecting my lips to his.

The last thing I remember before falling asleep was Jake's lips on mine.

Chapter Nine

When my alarm went off the next morning, it felt like I hadn't slept at all. I was so exhausted I couldn't even think straight. I went to turn off my alarm but was held in place by an arm. An arm? And just like that, last night came flooding back into my memory. I smiled as I looked over and saw Jake lying on his stomach beside me. He was even handsome with his cheek squished into the bed. I began to sit up but only made it up to my elbows before being pulled firmly into his side.

"Mmmm. Five more minutes." His eyes weren't even open yet, and he was so gosh darn cute. How could I say no?

"You have three," I laughed, "And then I have to go get ready for school."

"Only three? Then I guess I have to make the best of them." With one swift movement, I was looking up into his eyes. I wrapped my arms around his neck as he lowered himself down to connect his lips to mine.

"Emma! You had better be up already," my sister was practically shouting as she banged on my door. "Mom says she needs you to take me to school, and I don't want to be late! I just have to finish drying my hair." I froze. Oh my God! McKenzie and my parents were all just a door away from seeing Jake. Here. In my bed. "Emma! Hello?"

I shot up, bumping my head on Jake's chin in the process. "Yeah! OK. Got it! Ready in ten," I panicked, running my hand over where I had just inflicted pain. Then I looked over to see Jake doing the same thing.

"You OK? You sound like..."

"Fine, Kenzie. Just running late. Meet you downstairs, mmkay?"

"Alrightie. But you better hurry."

Jake was stifling a laugh as we heard her walk away. I swatted his arm and tried to sound stern, but just looking at him with his hair messy from just waking up made that very difficult. "You so cannot get caught in here. They would kill both of us. And I'm too young to die."

"Yeah, it would be kind of hard to date you if your parents killed you," he teased. He threw the covers back and got out of bed. I quickly faced forward and could feel the blush spread across my cheeks as he pulled his jeans on, then walked to my side of the bed.

Wait. When did his jeans even come off? Did he consciously sleep over last night?

145

"I love you, my blushing beauty." He kissed the top of my head, then walked over to my window, pausing to look back over at me before he climbed out. "Now hurry up and get ready. I can't wait to see you today," he shot me a wink and then he was gone.

Not ten seconds later my sister was bursting into my room, freaking out that I was still in bed. "OMG, Emma! I can't believe you are still not up! You have less than ten minutes until we need to be walking out the door, and I am not leaving this room until you are ready. You clearly cannot get motivated to get up and moving on your own. What is with you today? This is so not like you to be running this late?"

"Sorry, Kenz," I said smiling, "Just tired today I guess." At this point, I really didn't care about the big, sappy grin on my face or the fact that it took me longer than it should have to tear my gaze from the window and look at my sister.

She looked over and saw the window was still open. Her jaw dropped as she drug her gaze back over to mine, "Was Gabe here all night?"

"No. Guess I never shut the window last night. You know I can never get him to leave. Must have been so tired it slipped my mind." My voice was way too cheery. Kenzie was definitely going to catch on if I didn't start acting like the non-morning person that I really was.

"Uh, huh. Right." She cocked one of her eyebrows up and gave me a look. "I seriously can't believe you would do this to Jake. He is so perfect, and so cute, and clearly crazy about you."

A little taken aback by my sister's accusation, I kicked my legs out of the covers and started to get out of bed. How could she think I would ever cheat on Jake? On anyone for that matter? "I would never do anything to jeopardize what I have with Jake. I really like him. No, I'm in…" I paused as I slipped on my jeans from yesterday that were still on the floor, realizing that I was gushing.

"Oh my God, Emma. You love him. You're in love with Jake!" she squealed. "And oh." She glanced back over at the window, and I knew she knew. "You are so busted, Emma Crawford."

"Please don't tell mom," I begged as I walked over to grab a t-shirt from my closet and slipped it on.

I was twisting my hair into a bun when my sister crossed her arms. "What's in it for me?"

I looked over at her while I put the finishing touches on my hair. "Seriously? What about sister code, or I'll owe you when you inevitably need my help?"

"Yeah, whatever. Just remember this the next time I need a favor." She was all smiles, and I could tell she was enjoying every minute of this.

"Oh, I'll remember this all right. You know, Kenz, sometimes you can be a real pain in the butt." We both laughed, then I grabbed my flip-flops and we were out the door.

* * *

147

I was surprised when I saw Maya standing with Jake, Evan, and Gabe when I got to school. I thought that after yesterday, I was for sure going to have to track her down today. But there she was talking and laughing like everything was fine, doing what Maya does best, ignoring the problem and putting on a face to hide her true feelings. Yet this time everything was not fine, I was not fine with what went down yesterday. I was about to say something as I walked up, but Jake beat me to it.

"Morning, Blondie," Jake greeted, pulling me into him with a shit eating grin on his face. "You look tired today. Not get much sleep last night?"

Gabe immediately took the defense. "Come on, man. I wasn't even over there last night. So it wasn't me keeping her up this time."

"I believe you, bro," Jake smiled as he slapped Gabe on the back, causing my eyes to go wide and me to turn a dark shade of red. One glance at me, and it only took a moment for realization to sweep over everyone. I was so embarrassed and irritated that Jake had just handled that the way he did. He made it seem like a lot more happened last night than it did.

Maya looked over at me with wide eyes, knowing all too well a group reveal is not how you want everyone to find out the details of your relationship. "Emma. Emergency bathroom meeting. Now." She reached out for my arm, but I yanked it back.

Between sleep deprivation and everything that happened yesterday and just now, I snapped, "Are you

148

kidding me? So we are friends again? Now that my life isn't "oh so perfect"? News flash Maya; it doesn't work that way." In the back of my mind, I knew I should take a moment to stop and clear up any misconceptions, but I was on a roll.

Then I turned to Jake, "And seriously? So glad I could provide you with bragging rights. Looks like the joke's on me this morning." With that, I knew I had solidified what everyone was already thinking, but in the moment I didn't care.

I didn't bother looking at anyone else before turning and rushing off to Spanish class. Once I had I sunk down in a corner seat, I realized I forgot my book in my locker, but there was no way I was going back out to get it. Maya tried a few times to get my attention during class, but I ignored her. This time I was the one that needed a little space. Thankfully she seemed to understand that, or it just pissed her off, because she left me alone the rest of the day.

Jake texted me all morning, apologizing for how things went down and for being such a jerk. Right before lunch I told him to stop texting me and that I needed time to think. He texted back saying that he respected that and would be there whenever I was ready to talk.

I wasn't really hungry at lunch but knew I would regret not eating later; so I went through a drive-through and ate it when I got back to the school parking lot. I had never eaten lunch by myself before; it kinda sucked, but I was way too embarrassed to face any of my friends.

Once I'd had time to cool off, I wasn't sure what it was that made me freak out the way I did. All I knew is that

I was embarrassed about the entire thing. And that I was mad at Jake for making it seem like we had done more than we had. And that if we had done more than just kiss, that he felt like he could announce it to the whole freakin' group! And I was mad at Maya for acting like EVERYTHING was fine and then just assuming that I'd had sex with Jake – when I clearly haven't – though that's not what any of my friends currently think. Humph.

I managed to avoid everyone after lunch but had no idea how practice was going to go down. I was just so embarrassed about what happened earlier, mostly about how I acted. I contemplated telling coach I wasn't feeling well and taking a sick day. I knew he would believe me, and that it would totally work because I never missed practice even when I was a little sick.

I had just convinced myself that's what I was going to do – get through my last class and call coach after school – when I saw Jake standing by my locker. He looked like a mess. For a moment I felt bad for him, but then I remembered what he did this morning and brushed right past him.

"Emma, we need to talk." His voice was strained. Again, I had a second where I wanted to make it all better, but the anger came back too quickly.

"Jake, I have nothing to say to you." I didn't even look at him as I reached out to open my locker. But he was quicker. His hand slammed next to mine, preventing me from opening it. OK, now I was really mad. "Move Jake. I need to get my book and get to class. I don't want to be late."

"You're not going to class," he said firmly.

I whipped around and shot him a look. "Excuse me? You do not get to start telling me what I can and cannot do, Jake."

"We need to talk, Emma," He repeated with the same firmness in his voice.

"You're starting to cause a scene. Move and let me get my stuff so I can get to class."

"We can do this here or we can go to my truck, but you are not doing anything else until you hear me out. I am not losing you over a misunderstanding."

"Fine, I'll manage without my book." I turned and started to walk away.

"Why are you making this so difficult?" he grumbled loudly. Jake quickly closed the space between us, grabbed my bag and threw it over one shoulder, and me over the other.

"Jake, you are being such a jerk. This is ridiculous. Put me down!" I attempted to free myself but my efforts were a lost cause. By this point, most of the hallway had stopped to look at us with shocked faces.

"Quiet down, Emma. You're starting to cause a scene," he mimicked, using my own words against me. Not wanting to gain any more attention than we already had, I gave up and rested my chin in my hands as he carried me out of the building.

When we finally made it out to his truck, he tossed my bag in the bed, opened the back door, and set me down on the seat. "Like I said, we need to talk."

I smirked, "Like I said, I have nothing to say to you." I crossed my arms and refused to make eye contact with him.

"Damn it, Emma. You are so stubborn. That's one of the things I love about you. Do you hear me? I love you." He took my cheeks in his hands and forced me to look at him. I didn't say anything for a few seconds and neither did he. "I am so sorry about this morning, beautiful. I did not mean for things to happen the way they did. I'm such an ass. I don't know what came over me, but I just needed Gabe to know that he was not the only one who could crawl through your window. And then you turned so, so red. And everyone just assumed...then you got all mad and stormed off, confirming what everyone was thinking."

"Oh great. So this is all my fault now?" I steamed.

"No. No, of course not. It was a series of misfortunate events. But, Emma, I love you so much. I've been worried all day that I was going to lose you over this when I never meant for any of it to happen the way it did." He lowered his hands to my knees and dropped his head.

I took a minute to think about everything that he said. I already knew things wouldn't have gone down the way they did if I could have laughed it off and not freaked out. More importantly, after hearing him out, I believed him when he said he didn't mean for any of it to happen the way it did. So because I was being freaking emotional, I have tortured the both of us all day.

"OK," I finally said. He looked up at me with the saddest look on his face, which caused me to laugh. "I don't think you meant for everything to happen the way it did." His eyes got wider and a look of relief took over his face.

"I really didn't, babe, and I am so sorry that it did."

"Oh so it's babe now?" He looked at me questioningly. "Apparently you like B's. That's cool, everyone has a thing."

"Emma, what are you talking about?"

"Well first there was Blondie, and now apparently there's babe," I said matter-of-factly. "You know, I actually kind of like when you give me nicknames."

He smiled that perfect smile of his. "Oh, I can think of a whole bunch of things to call you." He slipped his hands around my waist. "Beautiful," he said as he kissed my lips. "Sexy." He peppered kisses across my jaw. "And my favorite, mine," he whispered, placing a kiss on my neck and sending chills throughout my entire body.

"Yours huh?" I teased, although there was no denying it. My heart was his. I was his, and I knew that there was no going back.

"Yes, mine." The possessiveness in his voice was causing my body to react, and this time I didn't care. I reached out for him and circled my arms around his neck. "Today, tomorrow, and forever," he whispered the last word so quietly that I couldn't quite make it out, but before I could ask him what he said, he claimed my lips with his.

Each time he kissed me I wanted – no – I needed him more. I began to scoot back into his truck and Jake moved with me, hopping in and shutting the door with ease. He kissed me so passionately I gave no thought to the fact that we were in the middle of the senior parking lot. I was officially starting to lose the little control I still had over myself when it came to Jake. That fact made me feel both nervous and exhilarated at the same time.

Chapter Ten

There was no point in walking into the last twenty minutes of class, so we decided to go to Sonic and get a drink before practice. I decided the first time I saw my friends again was going to be awkward no matter what, so it would be better to go to practice and get it over with. Plus, it helped having Jake with me to break the ice.

Jake and I got to practice after everyone else. When they saw us walk onto the courts hand in hand, we got a few nods and one forced smile that came from Gabe. The only person that wasn't making an effort to let me know all was well was Maya; she didn't even as much as look in our direction. Since I wanted to get through practice without any more incidents today, I followed Jake to a court to warm up instead of taking the spot by her.

The start of practice went smoother than I thought – much, much smoother. No one even mentioned what happened this morning. Even though at some point today, I want to clear up the details about what really happened.

When coach told us to take a lap around the school, I fell into my rhythm and didn't notice the person beside me until she spoke up. "Walk break?" she asked once we got to a spot coach could no longer see us.

I glanced over to see Maya jogging next to me. "No. I just want to finish this lap and get back to the courts. OK?" I phrased it as a question, but when I kept jogging it became clear that it was more of a statement.

Maya jogged ahead of me and I thought I was in the clear until she quickly turned and stopped right in front of me. "Not OK. Listen, Em. Stephen is getting worse. So, when everything happened the other day, I just lost it."

At the mention of her dad's name, I stopped dead in my tracks. "What? What happened? Did he hurt you?" I asked with genuine concern in my voice. I wouldn't put it past that man to lay his hands on either of them. Even before he started making both of their lives hell, something about him had always given me the creeps.

"No," she looked away, "but he shoved my mom and made her hit her head, and then told me it was my fault." She kicked a rock away from us and then looked right at me. "Em, that asshole told me it was my fault that he put his hands on my mom because I didn't know when to shut up. I hate him. I hate him so much. I wish she would just leave him." Tears were now pouring down her face, and I immediately wrapped her in a hug.

"I'm so sorry, Maya. About everything," I soothed as she cried. Tears welled up in my own eyes for hurt for my friend and for hatred of the man that was supposed to love and protect her.

She nodded into my shoulder and sniffed, "Me too." She took a step back and wiped her eyes. "You must think I'm a pretty shitty friend, huh?" she said with a forced laugh.

"Nah. You're not a shitty friend." I wiped a tear that escaped from my eye. "I don't know how you hold it together with everything that man puts you through," I offered a smile that she returned.

"Ya know, sometimes I wish so badly that we were kids again. When my biggest problem was scraping my knees when we would go roller skating, because there was no way in hell I would be caught in those tacky knee guards."

I laughed, remembering all the times Maya hurt herself on those stupid skates. "Those tacky knee guards would have prevented you from busting up your knees. That and slowing down or watching where you were going," I teased.

"Well. I was never too worried because you were always there to help me up," she said with a warm smile. "And share your skittles," she added with a smirk.

"I'll always be there to help you up, Maya." I reached out and squeezed her hand. "Always. Although, I may not always share my skittles."

She let out a small laugh. "Love you, Em."

157

"Love you too."

Knowing coach was not going to be happy that we were going to be the last two back, we immediately started jogging. Quickly. Falling in to a sprint when the courts were in sight. We were both completely out of breath by the time we made it back.

* * *

After practice, I was putting my stuff in my car when Maya leaned against the side. "So you and Jake, huh?" I looked up to see her wiggling both her brows with a stupid grin on her face.

"Oh, shut it!" I laughed. "There is no me and Jake. Not like that."

"OK," she giggled. "But just tell me one thing." Maya leaned closer with a serious look on her face. "Would you say he was more like this, or like this?" she said using her two pointer fingers to indicate a smaller or larger length.

"Maya! Oh my God! I just told you nothing happened! And even if it would have, I am not going to discuss the size of my boyfriend's..."

Maya cleared her throat just as Jake walked up behind me. "The size of my what?" he questioned, sounding amused.

I looked at Maya with wide eyes. "Nothing," I replied as heat rose to my cheeks, knowing he knew exactly what we were talking about.

"Well, I guess I'll leave you two to talk about...nothing." Maya looked from me to Jake with a smile that looked like she was fighting off cracking up. "Toodles." She wiggled her fingers at us as she sauntered off.

"So, I'd love to hear what you were going to say," Jake teased.

"Yeah. Not gunna happen."

"Meh. It was worth a shot." I rolled my eyes. "Don't you roll your eyes at me, Blondie," he said with a playful edge in his voice.

"Or what?" I challenged.

All of a sudden Jake reached out for me and pinned me against my Jeep with a sexy smirk on his face. "Or this." He connected his lips to mine, which caused those still in the parking lot to start whistling. He broke the kiss, and we both looked in the direction of the noise with huge smiles on our faces. With a breathy laugh, he rested his forehead on mine. "A few of my friends are going to my ranch this weekend for the long weekend. Any chance you would be able to go?"

"You have a ranch?"

"Yes, Emma," he chuckled.

"Sorry. I don't know why I was so surprised by that," I said sheepishly. I was a little embarrassed that was the first thing to come out of my mouth, but Jake didn't seem to mind.

"Do you think your parents would let you go?" he asked again.

"Away with my boyfriend? For the weekend? Are your parents going?"

"No."

"Um. That would be a big fat no. Like such a big no, I'm not even going to bother asking." Was he serious? Like anybody's parents would let their kid go away with a boyfriend or girlfriend for the weekend. Much less mine. It was such an absurd idea that I couldn't help but laugh.

Jake's brows furrowed. "What's so funny?"

The fact that Jake was so serious made me laugh even harder. "Really? Whose parents willingly let them go out of town with the person they're dating?"

"Mine," he said so matter-of-fact it caused me to stop laughing and look right at him.

"Seriously?"

"Eeek! Did he ask you?" Maya squealed as she came running up.

I still had a look of disbelief on my face when I turned to look at Maya. "You mean about the ranch?"

"Yes! It's going to be so much fun!" she squealed.

"Maya. You know my parents would never let me go."

"Duh. That's why we're going to do what we do when one set of our parents leaves town," she said simply.

"No. That's totally different. I am still in town then. What if they call and check up on me and figure out I skipped town?" I asked with panic in my voice.

"Chill out, Em. That is never going to happen. That would require our parents actually talking to each other. I

160

don't even think your parents have the number to my house."

She was right. They probably didn't. That was the one good thing about her jerk of a father. My parents were more or less in the loop about Maya's home situation, and I'm almost positive Maya's mom was aware of that fact. Therefore, neither side talked to the other more than they had to, which was at the occasional tournament her mom bothered to show up for. Because of that, any time one of our parents left town we would both say we were staying with the other for the weekend. Therefore, we had an entire house to ourselves for the whole weekend, and it was awesome!

"I don't know. It never seemed like a big deal when we were in town. But out of town? For a long weekend? There is just a lot that could go wrong. What if my parents ever talked to Jake's parents and it came out? I would be grounded until I was thirty."

"Do your parents even know each other?" Maya asked.

"No. But..."

"No buts, Em. They clearly are not going to meet before tomorrow, and, when they finally do, why would they be like oh what did y'all do for that long weekend a month ago?"

"Well that's a good point, but Jake does know my parents and I'm not going to make him have to lie to them."

"It's not something I would like to do," Jake chimed in, "but if it meant getting to spend the weekend with you at

161

the ranch, it would be worth bending the truth a little bit." He shrugged. "Plus, I could finally teach you how to shoot."

"OK, that's cheating. You know how badly I want to learn."

"Now you know how badly I want you to come this weekend, darlin'," he added with a sexy drawl.

"Oh, so you're resorting to that now are you?" I laughed as Jake smiled. I let out a sigh. "Fine. I'll ask my parents tonight if I can stay with Maya for the weekend. But if this gets out, I hope you two are OK with never seeing me outside of school ever again." I couldn't stop the smile from spreading across my face as Maya squealed and clapped her hands together.

"It won't, Em. This weekend is going to be so much fun!" Maya beamed.

It hit me then for the first time that Maya was a little too excited about me going away with Jake for the weekend. "Wait. Are you going too?"

"Pfft. Yeah. Evan asked me right before I ran back over here to you guys."

Exactly one hour and twenty-seven minutes later, I was sitting in my bowl chair with my knees to my chest calling Maya to let her know I was "staying with her" for the weekend.

"That's great, Em. I knew this wasn't going to be an issue. And why are you whispering?" She sounded totally normal. Not nervous at all. *How do I seem to be the only one who feels like my nerves are about to burst out of my chest like a swarm of butterflies?*

"Because we both know what we are really doing this weekend. Assuming your parents said yes." I was still whispering. I couldn't stop. It was like I was expecting my mom to swing open my bedroom door, at any moment, and tell me I was caught.

"You know they don't care. And, Em, you really need to chill out before your parents ask you why you're acting so weird. It's going to be fine. You'll see," she reassured me. In the back of my mind I knew she was right, but my nerves couldn't seem to get the memo. "Now go pack. Tell your mom that you are going straight to my house after school tomorrow. I don't trust how your little ball of nerves would handle swinging back by your house to get your stuff tomorrow after school.

"Good point. See you tomorrow." I was still whispering and could practically feel Maya rolling her eyes through the phone as she hung up.

* * *

Practice was optional on Friday because of the long weekend. So after school Evan, Maya, and I loaded up in Jake's truck while Heath, Spencer, and Spencer's girlfriend, Alli, loaded up in Heath's truck. We decided to leave the rest of our cars at school near the tennis courts since it could look like we were parked for the courts or the houses across the street.

As soon as we were pulling out of the school parking lot Jake turned on the radio, then reached over and laced our fingers together. He pulled my hand over, placed a kiss on the back of my hand, and then set our hands down on the center of my lap, letting his arm rest against my thigh. I looked over at him, and he gave me one of his perfect smiles before refocusing on the road with the most content look on his face. All the nerves in the world were worth chancing a weekend getaway with Jake.

I was so caught up in the excitement of this weekend that I almost didn't feel my phone vibrate, in my purse, against my foot. I instantly panicked, thinking it was going to be my parents; that they somehow knew and that I was so busted. I quickly reached down, grabbed my phone, and was flooded with relief at the sight of Gabe's name.

I was not about to put a damper on Jake's mood by answering Gabe's call. So I silenced the vibrations and slid my phone back into my purse, making a mental note to call him back when we got home on Monday.

Three hours and forty-five minutes later, we pulled off the main road and up to a big gate with an R at the top. Jake handed Evan a key and he hopped out of the truck to go unlock the gate. Jake pulled in, driving far enough to let Heath pull in behind us before stopping to wait for Evan to get the gate closed and climb back in the truck. We drove a few minutes up the road before a huge house with front porch lights on came into view.

"Damn, Jake," Maya said, leaning up from the backseat as we pulled up to the house, "Any other giant ass houses we need to know about?"

"Just this one," Jake chuckled, then looked over at me with a sexy grin. "Ready to go inside?"

"Yeah," I replied, trying not to make it obvious to everyone else in the car that just a look from him caused me to melt.

Jake gave me one more smile before hopping out of the truck and grabbing both of our bags. As we walked inside he threw my bag over his shoulder, freeing up one of his hands to take mine. "Come on, Blondie. Our room is this way," he said in a way that made my stomach do a flip.

A rush of excitement spread through me. I looked over at Maya, who gave me a wink and then slapped my butt as Jake led me toward our room.

"Looks like that means we're bunking together," Maya told Evan as we were walking away.

"Hell yeah," I heard Evan say before we turned down a hallway. There was definitely something going on between the two of them, and I was determined to make Maya spill before the weekend was through.

Jake walked to the end of the hall before stopping in front of a large, rustic, wooden door. He dropped my hand to open it, and then laced his fingers back through mine as he led me inside.

I let my eyes trace over the room, appreciating every unique detail along the way. "This place is like something you would see in a movie. Every little detail is just so...neat." There really was no other way to describe it. From the moment we pulled up, there was no denying that this place was special. Every little detail had been attended to, from the elaborate landscaping to the careful cracks in the wood paneling that had been stained to perfection. Every accessory I had seen so far made this place feel like the Upper East Side had met the country. It was an interesting combination but somehow fit together seamlessly.

Jake set our bags down and ran his hand through his tousled hair, taking a second to glance around the room. "Yeah, my mom is really into decorating." He made his way over to where I was standing, obviously not as entranced by this house as I was, and circled one of his arms across my lower back. "But I can think of a few things I'd like to do other than talk about my mom's decorations." He lowered his head so that his lips were inches from my ear. "I hope you brought boots, Blondie."

There was something different about the way he spoke, even the way he held me. His entire demeanor had changed. Maybe it was being at this place or just all in my mind. I couldn't put my finger on it, but something was definitely different.

"Who comes to a ranch and doesn't bring boots?" I smiled as my entire body warmed due to his close proximity and the way his thumb was tracing little circles on my lower back.

"Good point," he whispered huskily as he backed me up against the large king-size bed, causing my pulse to start racing. "You should probably change in to them then. You're going to need them for what we are about to do," he uttered into my neck.

"Is that," I sucked in a breath of air when his lips made contact with my neck, "so?"

We heard two girls squealing from the other room. Jake let out a frustrated growl before taking a step back. "Come on, Blondie. Sounds like everyone else is settled already." I quickly swapped my flip flops for boots and followed Jake out of our room.

We walked into the living room to see Maya and Alli running around the couch trying to avoid Heath, who had a small snake in his hands. Spencer was watching with amusement, and Evan was bent over with laughter. Jake took one look at the entire scenario and then threw his head back laughing. Apparently, he thought this was as humorous as Evan did. I had to admit it was quite amusing to see the both of them freak over a tiny garden snake. And before I could stop it, a small laugh escaped my lips.

"Emma, you wouldn't think this was so funny if this were a spider," Maya shouted.

"Spider, huh?" I looked to my left to see Jake standing with his arms crossed and brow lifted. "You realize Heath is more than likely going to try something now. I swear that guy just can't help himself."

"Yeah...I'm not too worried," I shrugged. "See, I have this boyfriend who I doubt would let him get close enough to try anything."

"Damn straight. Now hop on. We need to go outside." Jake turned so that his back was to me. When I didn't jump on his back right away, he looked over his shoulder. "Em, one way or another I'm carrying you out of this house. So you can either jump on my back or I can throw you over my shoulder."

I couldn't contain my giggle as I jumped up and he hooked an arm around each of my legs, securing me to him. "Jake, I'm wearing boots, you know, and it's not even that dark outside."

"Yes and you look adorable." He started walking as he glanced over to Heath tormenting the girls. "Heath, put that thing down and get outside and give me a hand, would ya?"

"You got it, man."

Jake carried me out to where a large outdoor kitchen was set up. He set me down and then cranked up the grill.

"Alright. What do you need me to do?" Heath asked as he walked up.

"Go around back and see what Sophie has stocked up for us. Grab whatever can be grilled," Jake instructed, while he raked a brush across the grill.

"On it."

I watched as Heath jogged off then turned my attention back to Jake. "Sophie?" I inquired.

"She keeps our house clean while we're gone and does the shopping for us so that we don't have to drive an hour to the closest grocery store once we get here. She's been with our family for as long as I can remember. She even used to babysit me and my sister sometimes when we were little," he explained.

168

"Right. Because who doesn't have a personal assistant that takes care of their second home," I teased.

Jake turned to face me, pointing the grill brush in my direction. "Is that sarcasm I detect in your voice?"

I placed my hands in my back pockets. "Nope. Nu-uh." I shook my head, fighting off a smile.

Jake lowered the brush and took a step toward me, closing the gap between us and placing a quick peck on my lips. "Whatever you say, babe...you like that nickname, right?" This time using a sarcastic tone himself. I rolled my eyes, and a grin stretched across his face as he turned back to the grill and finished preparing the surface.

When Heath showed back up, he had an assortment of items with him. So for dinner we had BBQ chicken, sausage, boudin sausage, and grilled corn. There was so much food I thought we'd have enough for today and tomorrow, but the boys had no trouble plowing right through all of it.

After dinner everyone pitched in cleaning up, so it took no time at all before we were all piled on the couch and chairs in the living room watching TV. Alli was the first to nod off. When Spencer said they'd see everyone in the morning, we all followed suit and headed to our own rooms.

Jake walked in our room, and I paused at the door – nerves creeping in for the first time today. Yes, I had slept in the same bed as Jake before but that was an accident. It was late; we had both sort of just fallen sleep. This was different. We were both walking in, knowing we were getting in the same bed, while we were away for the weekend

169

together. Were there expectations that went along with something like this? *Oh my God! I had not thought this through all the way.* Suddenly, all my nerves were stirring up and I reached for the door frame to steady myself. *Get it together, Emma. Why the heck am I suddenly so nervous?* I looked up to see Jake looking at me with a concerned expression.

"You OK, Em?" He walked over to me, grabbing both my cheeks with his hands, studying me with his eyes.

"Yeah," I lied, "I uh...um..." I swallowed before glancing over at the bed. Jake didn't miss any of it. His gaze followed mine, and when he turned back to me a soft smile broke across his face.

"Em, I can sleep on the couch if this makes you feel uncomfortable." He sounded so genuine and sincere that I immediately felt silly for having any doubts or worries about this situation. Of course he wasn't assuming things were just going to happen between us.

"No. Don't do that. Besides, we would catch crap the entire weekend if you did that."

He brushed his thumb across my cheek and gave me a kiss. "I'm going to grab a pillow, and then I'll see you in the morning." He turned to walk over to the bed.

I reached out and grabbed his arm. "No. Really, you don't have to do that. I want you to stay," I said, anxiously taking my lower lip in between my teeth. *Good Lord. What is my issue? I'm acting like a crazy person with split personalities.*

Jake glanced down at my lip and then once again met my gaze. "Are you sure, Em? Because I don't mind taking the couch. I don't care what anyone else thinks."

I have no idea why I was so freaking nervous earlier. This is Jake we are talking about. The boy I am in love with and have thought about doing a whole heck of a lot more with than just sleeping in the same bed. Whatever nerves I had left were completely gone, and I knew I had to find a way to convince him that I was serious when I said stay. Not knowing a better way to do that, I slid my arms around his neck and kissed him.

He was hesitant at first. But when I didn't pull away, he wrapped his arms around my waist and kissed me back. I began to move away from the door and he moved with me, closing the door behind us before pulling back to look at me. "Emma, you are the most confusing girl I have ever met," he grinned.

"Shut up and kiss me," I mumbled, stifling a laugh.

"Yes ma'am!" He connected his lips to mine, and I could feel him smiling against my mouth. When his smile faded, he deepened the kiss, running one hand up my back and gripping the nape of my neck. His touch caused my body to arch forward, pressing against him. "Mmm. Emma. You can't do things like that."

Yep. I bet I was super confusing. A moment ago I felt like my nerves were going to take over and now I was fine. More than fine. Jake had this way of calming me and giving me a surge of confidence I never thought I'd have.

"Like what? This?" I pressed into him again, causing him to let out a muffled groan before lifting me up, wrapping one leg around either side of him, and walking us over to the bed. He laid me down and gave me one more kiss before pulling away with a mischievous grin on his face. "What?"

"Just so you know. I am not sleeping with you tonight." He took a step away from the bed. "But I do plan on cuddling the crap out of you, so you should probably go get ready for bed," he finished with a satisfied grin.

"Wait. What?" I sat up on my elbows. What the heck just happened? Yeah, I was a little nervous about this earlier. OK, a lot nervous. But then I wasn't and then we started kissing. And it's not that I was expecting things to go that far tonight, but I guess I assumed it could happen. Then, he lays me down on his bed and flat out tells me he won't sleep with me. What the heck?

Jake chuckled. "You just want me for my body. And this," he said lifting up his shirt revealing his abs, "I'm not just some piece of meat, Emma."

I fell back in laughter. "Oh my God. You did not. You're such a girl!"

He collapsed over me and planted a kiss on my lips. "But seriously, you should go get ready for bed."

He was serious? He really doesn't want me? Even though I wasn't one hundred percent planning on it earlier, I, for sure, wanted to know why he wasn't. "Seriously? Is there a reason you are so easily dismissing me?"

"Yes, seriously." He reached up and ran his thumb over my bottom lip, letting his eyes linger there before looking back into my eyes. "And trust me, I am not easily dismissing you. You were hesitant earlier, Em, and I don't want there to be any hesitation before we are together for the first time."

My cheeks flushed at his words. And wouldn't you know that everything he said just made me want him more? "I'm not hesitant now," I countered in a small voice.

He smiled down at me and then kissed the tip of my nose. "Tonight, we sleep. But tomorrow, no promises." He winked at me, then climbed off the bed.

Knowing I wouldn't be able to change his mind, I got up and walked over to my bag to get my toiletries and then walked to the attached bathroom to brush my teeth. I had just put my toothbrush in my mouth when Jake walked in wearing only boxers. I don't know why, but I just wasn't expecting that and I almost choked on toothpaste when I saw him. He gave me a nod, and the smile on his face let me know how much he was enjoying this. Two could play at this game.

I quickly finished brushing my teeth and walked back into our room to change into my PJs. I opted for a pair of boy short panties and a snug fit spaghetti strap top. I had my back to the bathroom door, but I knew when Jake came back in the room because I heard him suck in a breath of air when he saw me. I smiled to myself before I turned around. "Ready for bed?"

Jake watched as I casually walked over to the bed and climbed under the covers. A few seconds later, he climbed in after me, pulling me into him as he snaked an arm around my waist. "You're trying to kill me, aren't you?" he whispered against my neck.

All I could do was smile. Two could definitely play this game. He may have not realized that he had just started a war, but tomorrow it was on. I drifted off to sleep loving that I had the upper hand.

Chapter Eleven

I dreamed that someone was calling my name. No, not someone, Maya. But there were other voices too. Wait...there's my name again. Followed by laughing. I opened my eyes to see Maya and Evan standing at the foot of the bed. "Good morning, sunshine," she sang.

"Oh no." I covered my head with my pillow. "Morning people, you're both morning people!"

"Stop moving. It's too early," Jake murmured in a sleepy haze as he rolled onto his side, pulling me into him.

Jake clearly was not yet aware that we had an audience, and it's a shame that we did. He is just so cute in the morning. All I wanted to do was roll over and kiss him. Instead, I did my best to pull away from him.

"Em, stop it," he whined, fighting me into his side. Realizing I was making it worse, I gave in and sheepishly let him pull me into him. I sunk into his side as both Maya and Evan lost it.

"Em, stop it," Evan mocked, causing the two of them to laugh harder.

Jake's eyes shot open. "What the hell, man?" He sat up as he scratched the back of his head.

"Dude. It's nine thirty. Are we going shooting or what?" Evan asked.

Jake checked the time on his phone. "Exactly, it's nine thirty. Couldn't we have waited an hour?" He glanced over at me and gave me a groggy grin.

"Holy crap! He's less of a morning person than you, Em," Maya chimed in, a little too perky.

Jake looked from Maya to Evan. "Oh no."

"Yep," I replied, knowing exactly what he was talking about.

"Morning people. Both of them," he said as though he were in shock.

"Yep," was all I could say.

Jake took a moment to contemplate our recent discovery, then grabbed one of the pillows from behind us and chunked it at them. "Get the hell out! And leave the rest of us normal people alone." He laid back down and pulled me into him.

"Looks like you two are going to need a minute," Maya said again in her overly perky tone. She grabbed Evan's hand and pulled him out of the room, closing the door behind them. Not two seconds later, she popped her head back in. "But seriously, we're leaving in ten. OK. Bye."

The door closed again and Jake groaned, "They're not going to leave us alone, are they?"

"Nope," I said popping the P.

Jake let out a frustrated sigh, "Alright then. After you." He flipped back the covers and gestured for me to go first.

"Me? Why do I have to go first?"

A sexy smirk took over his face as he reached out and ran his fingers under the hem of my top. "Like I said, no promises today." My jaw dropped and he shot me a wink, then climbed out of bed and began to dig clothes out of his bag.

"Oh, it's on! Brace yourself, sir, because you don't know what you're up against." I scrambled out of bed and threw on the first thing I grabbed out of my bag. Then we both walked out and met everyone else our two human alarm clocks woke up.

After a muffin and a few rounds of coffee, we were on the back of four wheelers riding out to where we were going to shoot. My first few attempts were awful. Jake watched me intently as I took my first few shots, then he fixed my stance and the position of my hands before telling me to aim again. I hit the edge of the target this time. I was so excited that my hands went straight up in the air, cueing Jake to rush over, grab the gun, and tell me to be more careful. He really does take gun safety seriously. By the time we were packing up, I had hit the target dead-on three times and I was dang proud of myself.

On the way back to the house, I remembered that we were supposed to be having an "unofficial" war. Jake had been so serious when he was teaching me to shoot, I

177

had completely forgotten about our little competition. I decided I had better step up my game.

Jake was driving our four wheeler so I slid a little closer, removing any gap that was between us, and pressed myself against him. His back went rigid, and I awarded myself my first unofficial point. "Point Emma," I said out loud, knowing he couldn't hear me over the sound of the four wheeler.

Jake slowed down until we fell behind everyone else. When we finally parked the four wheeler, the rest of the group had gone inside to get lunch. Jake helped me off and then pulled me into him. I had definitely gotten to him. He hovered his lips over mine. "Emma," he breathed. He ran his thumb over my jawline, turning my head as he lowered his lips to my neck, stopping right before he made contact. He blew a breath down my neck, causing a shiver to run down my spine and a small gasp to escape my lips. He raised his lips to my ear and whispered, "Point Jake."

He stepped back wearing that sexy smirk. What the heck? He totally heard me award myself a point earlier. All of that was just to get a rise out of me. "OK." I gave him my best game face. "Point Jake. But I hope you enjoyed that because that's the last one you're going to get today." I turned and started to walk toward the house, throwing a little extra hip into every step.

When we got inside, sandwich stuff had been pulled out onto the center island in the kitchen. Everyone was either sitting and eating their sandwich or still in the process of making one.

"Bout time. I was worried you two got lost," Maya teased as she put the finishing touches on her sandwich.

I walked over to where she was and started making my own sandwich. "Jake here started driving the pace of a turtle."

"Yeah, I noticed. Weird how that happens."

Normally Maya teasing me would have made my cheeks turn bright red, but I was preoccupied with beating Jake so I was only half listening. "Mmhm. Yep." I scanned the counter, obviously distracted. I picked up the mayonnaise and a piece of bread.

"Em, that's mayo. You don't even like..."

"Here, Maya, hold this for a sec." I quickly shoved a piece of bread in her hand. "Oh shoot!" I blurted out, after squeezing mayo onto a part of her hand that wasn't touching the bread. "My bad. Totally missed the bread."

"Eww! Em. What the..."

I cut her off again, grabbing her hand and palming my butt. "Maya! Why would you do that? You got mayo all over me!" I grabbed a paper towel and looked over both my shoulders like I was trying to see where all the mayo got on my shorts.

I walked over to the other side of the counter where Jake was standing and pouted, "Maya just got this crap all over me. I was going to wear these again. Can you please help? I can't see where all of it is." I gave him one more frustrated look before turning toward the counter and resting my forearms on the granite while bending over so he could see where all the "mayo" was. "Can you see it?" I whined.

"Yeah, Em. It's everywhere. Hold on, give me that paper towel. Maya, why the hell would you do this?"

Maya leaned back against the opposite counter eyeing me as she spoke with an amused grin, "I just don't know what came over me." She took a bite of her sandwich and watched as Jake attempted to clean off all the mayo.

I handed Jake one more paper towel and knew he wouldn't be needing another one as he let his hand slowly move across my backside one last time, lingering a little longer than needed.

"Alright. We got most of it," he let out in a strained tone.

I turned around to face him. "Thanks, Jake. I really appreciate it." A smile tugged at the corners of his mouth as I slid my arms around him to give him a hug and then leaned up to whisper in his ear, "Point Emma."

I began to pull out of his arms while realization swept over his face. "Oh you want to fight dirty, do you?" I gulped as I strained to free myself from his grip, but he was quicker and stronger. Once he had a solid grip on me, he threw me over his shoulder. "Alright then, Blondie. Let's fight dirty!"

"Jake!" I shrieked, while tirelessly trying to free myself. "When are you going to stop hoisting me over your shoulder and carrying me places?"

"Whenever you stop giving me a reason to," he chuckled. At the door, Jake stopped and turned toward the kitchen. "Grab a victim guys, we've got a bit of a walk."

"Do it and die," Maya threatened Evan as Jake opened the door.

Realizing my efforts to escape were futile, I once again resorted to resting my chin in my hands as Jake walked us outside. I watched through the door as Alli squealed when Spencer snatched her up and fell in line behind us. Maya, on the other hand, was shooting daggers at both Heath and Evan, silently warning both of them on the way out the door and the entire time we were walking.

I couldn't see where we were going, but I watched as the ground turned from manicured lawn to solid dirt. The air also went from fresh with a hint of flowers to a pungent scent that matched the surroundings. It felt like we had been walking forever when Jake finally stopped. "Am I finally getting too heavy for ya there, cowboy?"

"Not even close. Evan, help a guy out, would ya?" Jake called out as he nodded to something in front of him. I tried to turn and get a peek at what he was nodding at, but all I could see was the side of what looked like a barn. "Em, would you stop fidgeting? You'll see soon enough."

A knowing grin spread across Evan's face as he eagerly agreed. I knew something was wrong as soon as Maya started to back away, and then I heard it turn on. "Evan, don't you dare!"

"Oh, don't be such a baby, Em. It's just a little water. And you did ask me to help you clean all the mayo off, didn't you? Now what kind of boyfriend would I be if I didn't help you out?" He tightened his grip around me. "Go ahead, man. Let's make sure she gets nice and clean."

I let out a scream as soon as the water hit my skin. It was so cold. I started squirming more furiously than I had earlier. As soon as I could get down from here they were so dead, both of them.

The water made it harder for Jake to hold on to me. He eventually lost his grip, bellowing over in laughter once I was free. "Point Jake," he choked out between laughs. I would deal with him later. For now, I had to get that dang hose away from Evan and off of me. I eagerly took a step forward toward Evan, not thinking about the ground also being wet – until I slipped back into Jake, knocking us both down into what was now mud.

"Dude. Evan. We got a dry one over here," Spencer prodded.

"Well then, let me help you out with that," Evan moved the hose from me to Alli, who broke out into a fit of giggles. "Spence, move her over here. That way neither one of them can get too dry."

Jake was still on my hit list, but when I heard that the hose was coming back Evan became my top priority – again. Plus, Jake already had mud on his backside and that would do for now. I scrambled up, being more careful with my footwork than I had earlier, and went straight for Evan. I made sure to sling some mud back with my foot at Jake as I moved forward. "Maya! A little help here!" As soon as my words were out, Evan moved the hose back toward me and began alternating the water flow between Alli and I.

"Nah. Looks like you got it handled over there, Em!" Maya proclaimed loudly as I heard Jake, a little too late, come up behind me.

"Oh no you don't," Jake had a playful edge to his voice as he wrapped his arms around my waist. "You got me all covered in mud. The least I can do is return the favor." He wrestled me down to the ground before smearing mud on my cheek.

"Maya!" I screamed.

"Fine, bitch. I'm coming!" She tried her best to sound annoyed but even she couldn't choke back all of her laughter.

"Go for the hose!" I yelled, while trying to stop Jake from smashing a glob of mud on my chest.

"What?"

"Get the freakin' hose, Maya! The hose!"

I knew she heard me when Evan started shouting, "Hey. Heh, heh, heh, heh, heh, hey! One step closer and..."

"I've been hit!" There was no hiding the shock in Maya's voice. "Evan, surrender the damn hose!"

"Never!" he shouted. "Holy crap! She got it! We lost the hose! Repeat, we lost the hose!"

At his confession, Jake turned his attention toward Evan and chunked a handful of mud at him. "Son of a...Jake! We are supposed to be on the same team, moron!"

"Hey!" Alli piped up. "Heath doesn't have a drop of mud or water on him."

We all stopped and looked over at Heath. Sure enough, he was totally clean. Too clean. Before he could protest, Jake threw a glob of mud his direction that hit him in the back of the head.

"Seriously?" Heath barked, whipping around to face Jake and me. "Who threw that?"

Without missing a beat, Jake pointed at me and shrugged innocently. My jaw dropped and I gasped, "Liar! I can't believe you just threw me under the bus!"

Once Heath was involved, it turned into an all out girls versus guys muddy, water war; although, I'm pretty sure Jake was throwing mud at whoever was close to him. When everyone else picked up on that little fact, it turned into a free for all.

I don't know how long we had all been engaged in our mud war, but someone let out a catcall sort of whistle, cueing the rest of us to stop. I looked around and found Maya laying face up in the mud with her arms wrapped around Evan's neck. Both of them were looking into each other's eyes and wearing big, goofy grins. If I didn't know any better, I would say that the two of them just kissed.

Realizing they had an audience, Evan climbed off Maya and then helped her up. When Maya looked over at me, I raised one eyebrow and gave her a questioning look. The smile on her face grew and confirmed my suspicion. That little tramp! I can't believe she didn't tell me.

After everyone got over the spectacle of those two, we all glanced around and got a good look at each other for the first time. We looked ridiculous. There was mud everywhere.

"All I'm saying is all this mud slinging made me work up an appetite," Spencer said. "Plus, Alli needs a shower." He made a show of sniffing his girlfriend and then waving his hand in front of his nose, which earned him a playful shove.

"I could definitely eat. Someone didn't allow me to eat my sandwich earlier." Jake pulled me into him and kissed me square on the lips before I could protest. "But first we shower. Trust me when I say that none of you want the wrath of my mother to come upon you for tracking mud in her house," he laughed and then motioned for me to hop on his back, a request with which I readily complied.

By the time we got back to the house most of the mud on us had dried, but Jake still insisted we take off our shoes and leave them by the door. I tried to hop down so I could remove my shoes, but Jake tightened his grip, preventing me from slipping down. He motioned for me to stick one leg out at a time, and then he removed each of my shoes. We all walked as gingerly as possible back to our rooms so that we didn't get the floors any dirtier than they had to be.

I assumed Jake would put me down when we got back to our room, but he didn't. He walked in, shut the door with his foot, and then went straight through to the bathroom. Again, he shut the door with his foot then leaned slightly forward to keep me on his back as he turned the lock. The sound of the click caused my pulse to race.

Neither of us had said a word since we walked into our room, and I prayed he couldn't hear my heart beating frantically in the silence. *Stupid betraying body, and all because of one little click.*

He walked us over to the counter and turned around to set me down before turning on the shower to let the water heat up. When he walked back to me the look on his face let me know what he was thinking, and I bit my lip in anticipation. *Breathe, Emma. Slow. Deep. Breaths.* He placed one hand on each side of me on the counter and then leaned his forehead against mine, pressing against my legs with his body. My legs seemed to fall open on their own accord, allowing him to sink closer to me and causing me to suck in a breath.

I wrapped both arms around his neck and he lowered his lips until they were inches from mine. "I swear if you say point Jake, I will never speak to you again." I whispered breathlessly.

"Shut up and kiss me," he murmured against my lips.

I smiled at the use of my own words, and then did exactly what he asked. I connected my lips to his, and he instantly deepened the kiss. I tangled my fingers into his hair and was suddenly brought back to the reality of the situation. "Jake, there is dried mud everywhere," I laughed.

"I guess we're gunna have to fix that," he countered in a husky rasp, causing my giggles to fade. He secured me to the front of him and walked us over to the shower, opened the door, and stepped in, closing the door behind him. He walked us until my back was pressed firm against the wall and then crashed his lips into mine.

I no longer cared where there was dry mud. He kissed a trail across my jaw and then down my neck, sending my mind once again into that blissful, hazy, fog. I wiggled my legs until he let them drop and then adjusted my hands at the bottom of his shirt, tugging it up before I lost my nerve. He quickly shrugged out of it, making me feel braver and more eager than I had before. With my newfound audacity, I reached down and grabbed my own shirt, pulling it up and over my head in one swift move. Then, I reached back, unhooked my bra, and let it fall to the floor.

His eyes instantly went wide and he sucked in a sharp breath. He took a step forward, causing me once again to have my back against the wall, and then placed one hand on either side of me. His eyes took their time scanning down my chest before slowly coming back up to meet mine.

I silently took pleasure in the obvious effect I was having on him. Not wanting it to stop, I leaned forward until my lips met his and then reached out and hooked my fingers in his belt loops – pulling him closer. As soon as my bare chest hit his, he let out a low growl before wrapping one hand around the nape of my neck and the other around the small of my back. He secured me firmly to the front of him as he kissed me, only stopping when I sunk my thumbs into the top of his jeans and began to pull down.

187

"Emma," he let out in a throaty whisper, grasping both sides of my face and looking into my eyes. "You don't have to do that."

I took my bottom lip in between my teeth trying to decide if I was brave enough to follow through with what I so desperately wanted. *It's now or never. Deep breath.* I smiled a small smile and pressed my chest into him as I whispered in his ear as seductively as I could, "I thought today there were no promises."

He gulped, "Are you sure, Emma?"

I placed a kiss on his neck and let my lips spread in to a smile before leaning back and letting my shorts fall to the shower floor.

His eyes drank me in as they moved over my almost completely bare body. "Beautiful. You're beautiful," he whispered. "I plan on taking my time with you. I don't ever want you to forget our first time." His words alone caused my stomach to do a flip, but when he began running a soapy loofah over my body, gently cleaning all the mud off, I thought my heart might stop. "Perfect," he murmured against my neck once every inch of me was clean, sending a chill down my spine.

Nerves rose up my chest as I reached out and took the loofah, planning on wonderfully tormenting him the same way he had me. When my fingers wrapped around his to pull the loofah from his grasp, the corners of his mouth stretched into a smile. I ran my hand over his back and down his chest, stopping when my fingers hit the top of his soaked jeans, and let the loop of the loofah slip around my wrist. Using both my hands, I managed to easily undo the button, causing Jake to clamp his mouth shut. He reached out and braced himself against the wall as I tugged his jeans down, and then he slowly stepped out of them as I stood back up. He let out a groan as I ran the loofah over the rest of him and barely let me finish cleaning him off before reaching down and taking hold of both of my arms to once again pin me against the wall.

He crashed his lips to mine and slid his arms around the small of my back, pulling me back with him until I was directly under the water. I never would have imagined that kissing someone while they shampooed your hair could be so sensual until I experienced this with Jake. Once he was finished, I eagerly returned the favor.

When I was done, he wrapped me tightly in his arms and kissed me until I was breathless. "Don't move," he uttered, hopping out of the shower and reappearing with a towel in hand. "Turn off the water, Emma."

I turned the handle, shutting off the water, and took the few steps that closed the gap between us and into the towel that Jake held open. "Arms up, Em." I lifted my arms and he wrapped the towel around me, tucking the end in so that it would stay in place before lacing his fingers through mine and stepping out to lead us into the bedroom. He walked us over to the door. No sooner than he had turned the lock, he was pulling me into his chest and crashing his lips into mine.

He had both hands gripping each side of my face as he backed us into the wall – not once breaking the kiss. I ran my hands down his back, digging my fingers into his skin as I attempted to pull him closer, needing him closer. My head fell to the side as he dropped his lips to my neck, causing my back to arch forward and a moan to escape my lips. Jake let out a low growl and placed one hand against the wall while gripping my rear with the other, pulling me forward until my body was again fully pressed against him.

A nervous adrenaline surged through me as I snaked my hand between our bodies and pulled my towel free. Jake stepped back just enough to let it fall to the ground before pressing his chest back into mine. Placing both his hands on the wall, he lowered his lips to my ear. "I love the way your skin feels pressed up against mine," he breathed. "It drives me the best kind of crazy."

His words caused a smile to tug at the corners of my mouth while I reached up and circled my arms around his neck, kissing him as I pressed up on my toes. He must have known exactly what I was thinking because in one swift motion he was lifting me up, allowing me to secure my legs around his waist and then reconnecting my lips to his. My hands formed fists in his hair as I kissed him with everything that I had. Eventually, he walked us over to the bed, and I broke the kiss so that he would let me slide down once he had stopped. Before I lost my nerve I reached down and shimmied out of my panties, silently praying he couldn't hear my heart that was now beating incredibly fast.

Jake looked like he was in awe while his eyes gazed up and down before once again closing the distance between us. He cupped my cheeks with his hands and lowered his lips to mine. "I love you, Em," he murmured against my lips. "I don't know how it happened, but from the moment I met you I knew I would never be the same."

My entire body warmed as he kissed me. If I had thought my mind was in a haze before, I don't even know what you would call what it was in right now. Time seemed to slow as Jake reached down and removed the last piece of clothing that stood between us. All I knew for sure was that there was nothing I wanted more as he pressed his lips against mine and lowered us to the bed.

Chapter Twelve

After dinner, Maya insisted we build a campfire. She was convinced that there had to be some kind of unwritten rule about ranches and campfires going hand in hand. Alli squealed in delight at the idea, and I found myself rolling my eyes at her reaction.

It's not that she isn't super nice, it's just that somehow she keeps finding a way to redefine perky. I honestly don't know how Spencer keeps from putting a muzzle on her every other minute. I didn't realize I was gawking at her until Maya broke me out of my train of thought.

"Hello? Em? Marshmallow hunt? Yes?" She snapped her fingers, cueing me to listen to what she was going on about.

"Marshmallows? What?" I craned my neck to focus on Maya as my brain attempted to piece together what she was saying.

"Good Lord. Jake said that there might be marshmallows somewhere in the pantry. Help me look while the boys build the fire?"

"Well, don't just stand there," I teased. "We have marshmallows to find." I jumped up and walked toward the kitchen with Maya in tow.

"Anything you care to share, love? You've been quite distracted ever since we got all cleaned up," she pried with a suspicious stare.

I opened the pantry door and motioned for her to walk in first. She watched me curiously as she walked by. "Speaking of sharing." I closed the door to the pantry and then crossed my arms as I leaned back against it. "You have some explaining to do. Now spill."

Her expression turned into a wicked grin. "Moi?" She gestured to herself with her usual dramatic flare.

"Uh, don't even. You, ma'am, know exactly what I am talking about."

"It was just a kiss, Em. It didn't mean anything. Evan and I are just friends."

"Mmmhmm. And is Evan aware that you are just friends?"

She let out a sigh as she gazed over to one of the pantry shelves and adjusted a can of green beans. "He knows how I feel about Dylan, and we've talked about it. We agree that we are better as friends."

"Y'all agreed or you did?" I pressed.

"Will you stop with the third degree? We agreed, OK? It was just a kiss."

I could tell by the look on her face that it most certainly was not just a kiss, but I decided to leave it alone. She clearly is not ready to discuss whatever it is that is going on. "OK." I held my hands back, signaling my surrender. "I'm just saying; it looked like a whole heck of a lot more."

"Em!"

Laughing, I dodged the package of hamburger buns that she threw at me, then we both focused on searching for the marshmallows.

"Seriously? How are we supposed to find one little package of marshmallows in this thing? They could be anywhere."

"No freaking kidding," I let out.

We both sank against the back wall as we realized for the first time just how big this walk-in pantry was. As our eyes scanned the room that was bigger than my closet at home, I decided this was about to be more of a treasure hunt than a simple marshmallow-finding mission.

"Alright, let's start from the bottom and work our way up," she suggested.

What felt like ten minutes later, we admitted defeat and walked out of the pantry to rejoin the group outside. We were almost out of the kitchen when Maya piped back up.

"By the way, don't think for a second that I didn't notice your question dodge earlier. I know for a fact something happened with you two because it took y'all longer than anyone to "clean up", and Jake hasn't been able to keep his hands off of you." I snapped my head in her direction. "Oh yeah. I noticed. So tell me...did you?" The betraying smile that broke out on my face said it all. "Ahhh! I knew it!" she screamed as we stepped through the door.

"Maya. Oh my God. Quiet down. I don't want the whole freakin' group to know," I hissed.

She was grinning like an idiot. "You got it, boss. These lips are sealed." She zipped her lips and then flicked away the key. "So how was it? Are you sore?" she whispered.

"Maya!"

"OK. Got it," she said clearly amused, "But you know you are not going to be able to keep it from me forever. And I can't wait to hear all the juicy details!"

I stopped and looked directly at her. "Seriously? Don't make me get a muzzle for you too." Maya looked at me like she had no idea what I was talking about. "Don't act like you haven't thought about muzzling Alli yourself. You forget how well I know that evil mastermind of yours, my dear." Maya busted out laughing, falling forward and having to catch herself on her knees.

"Touché, my friend," she laughed.

"And maybe I am a little sore," I whispered.

"Ahh! It's literally going to kill me until you spill all the dirty little details!"

"And yet, I think you'll somehow survive."

"Bitch," she muttered under her breath.

"I heard that," I laughed.

195

Giggling, she threw her arm over my shoulder. "Come on. Let's get back over there. I'm sure by now Jakie is going through withdrawal and needs his Emma fix."

I rolled my eyes as we began walking back toward the group. "Remind me again why I claim you as my best friend?"

"Because you love me." She put her head on my shoulder and walked her fingers up my arm.

"Right."

The fire was going strong by the time we rejoined everyone with the news that the marshmallows were a no-go. After the initial letdown of not getting more food, the boys resorted to finding random things to throw in the fire. It became an all out competition about who could find the item that would burn the fastest.

In the middle of all the chaos, I stopped and watched Maya with Evan for a second. She was genuinely having a good time and seemed happier than I had seen her in a while. There was definitely something starting between those two, and I think the only person who didn't see it was Maya.

* * *

There were no nerves this time when we all separated for bed. I was actually looking forward to lying next to Jake, who greedily snatched me up and draped his arm over me after pulling the covers up over us. As soon as

I closed my eyes, Jake began to lightly run his finger in little circles over the side of my hip.

"Jake, there is no way I am going to be able to sleep if you keep doing that."

"So I probably shouldn't do this either?" He placed a soft kiss on the sensitive spot right below my ear that caused goose bumps to break out across my skin.

"I'm not sure you're understanding the severity of this situation," I teased. "You see, I happen to be a sleeper. And as much of me that wants to turn around and kiss you, a bigger part of me is currently much more attracted to the sleep option."

"And what happens if I don't let you give into the latter?" I could hear the smile in his voice as he let his fingers trickle up and down my side.

I turned to face him, "Bad, bad things. Murderous things."

Jake chuckled and then placed a kiss on my forehead. "Alright, Blondie. I see your point." I began to turn back around, thinking he consented to letting me sleep. I was barely able to turn because in an instant Jake had me on my back, hovering over me wearing a sexy grin. "But I think I'll take my chances." He bent down and pressed his lips to mine, and wouldn't you know my stupid, betraying body was on his side.

* * *

I woke up the following morning the same way I had the day before. Voices. The difference was this time they were accompanied by knocks and coming from the other side of the door. I sat up and looked at Jake, whose eyes were still closed, as I began to process what was happening. Jake's lips broke into a grin.

"Come back, Em. I sleep so much better when you're tucked in my arms."

"Trust me, nothing sounds better than sleep right now, but by the time I lay down those two are going to come barging in," I half whined.

Still refusing to open his eyes, Jake reached up with one arm and pulled me into him. "Nope," he nuzzled into my neck. "I locked the door last night, so we are safe to sleep and stay in this bed all day if we want to."

I relaxed when I realized those two freakin' alarm clocks of human beings couldn't enter my chamber of sleep. "Good, because I feel like I need at least eight more hours."

"Someone is grouchy this morning," Jake said with a small laugh.

"Yeah. Well, I did try to warn you that your own personal safety was at stake if I didn't get an adequate amount of sleep." I was now full on whining but was too tired to care.

"You're adorable when you're cranky," he mused.

"I hate you."

Jake chuckled as he adjusted his head on the pillow, pulling me firmly against him. "Go back to sleep, Emma. You are a little scary when you're tired."

I didn't protest. I shut my eyes, and as soon as I felt Jake's breathing even out, I drifted back to sleep.

The next time I woke up, I had no idea how long I had been out. It felt like I had been asleep for hours, but the bacon scent that was assaulting my nostrils told a different story. I reached over and grabbed my phone off the nightstand and checked the time.

10:00

I realized everyone else was probably just getting up as well and making breakfast. I looked over at Jake to find him still out cold. Leaning down, I slowly began to place kisses all over his face. When I placed my lips on his, I could feel him smiling and knew he was awake.

"Mmm. I could wake up like this every morning," he spoke, wrapping his arms around me. Then he squinted one eye open, "Unless scary Emma is still out there. In that case, I may just hide under the covers."

"I got more sleep. So you're safe...for now."

"Is that bacon?" Both of Jake's eyes were wide open, and I couldn't hold back my smile over how easily he was distracted once he smelled the food.

"Smells like it."

"Then what are we waiting for?" Jake jumped out of bed and dug a pair of sweatpants out of his bag: the kind that set right above his butt, allowing you to appreciate every abdominal muscle on display above them. If my stomach wasn't so busy telling me that I was hungry, the rest of my body would have attempted to lure him back to the bed.

We walked into the kitchen to find Heath coming in from the other hall at the same time we were. Everyone else had found a seat around the large island watching Maya cook up eggs and bacon while sipping on their cups of coffee. Upon that observation, I immediately found the coffeepot and poured myself a cup. I was leaning against the counter, enjoying my first sip when I realized everyone was still in PJs except for Maya and Evan. In fact, it looked like they had gone for a run...or something.

"What time did you two get up?" I asked Maya at the same time Evan hopped up and offered to help, taking over the eggs.

She kept her focus on the bacon she was flipping over. "Oh, I don't know. A couple hours ago maybe?"

"Uh huh," I let out slowly, "I see." I watched as the two of them finished cooking breakfast. They were too occupied with each other to even pick up on the fact that I was really asking why they were wearing athletic clothes and why Maya had grass in her hair while neither one of them appeared to have broken a sweat. I watched them intently as I sipped on my coffee until they told everyone to make a plate.

I couldn't tell you what happened over breakfast because I was too busy watching those two canoodle each other. I almost dropped my fork at one point when Maya literally fed bacon to Evan. Like. Fed. Him. That girl was either lying to herself or lying to me because I have never seen her act so lovey-dovey with anyone. Not even Dylan.

When everyone got up from the table, I followed Jake back into our room. "Did you notice anything weird between Maya and Evan?" I asked once the door was closed.

"So that's where you were," he teased, while grabbing a fresh shirt from his bag.

"What?"

Jake chuckled and walked over to me as he pulled the shirt over his head and then kissed the top of my forehead. "You were completely checked out at breakfast. I tried to get your attention a few times before I realized you were in your zone. You do that sometimes when you're really focused," he smiled.

"Oh," I blushed, "I didn't mean to ignore you." I didn't even realize this was a regular thing for me. *I wonder how often I just "check out" around people. Around Jake.*

"Don't apologize for being you, Em. Don't ever apologize for doing the little things that make you so perfectly Emma." The way he was looking at me caused me to turn a deeper shade of red.

How is it that Jake seems to know me better than I know myself? And why does that make me feel like I love him more than I already do?

"So, are you going to change or do you plan on going in that?"

"Change for what?"

Jake let out a small laugh, "Town. We decided at breakfast to go into Fredericksburg for the afternoon."

"Right. Of course." I turned to my bag and pulled out a shirt and pair of shorts.

I quickly changed and then ran a brush through my hair, throwing it up into a ponytail before putting on a little makeup. I had just applied a coat of lip gloss when I realized Jake was leaning against the door frame watching me.

"Beautiful," he said when my eyes met his, sending a rush of warmth through my body. "Now come on, Blondie, there is an ice cream place in town you have to try," he finished with that perfect smile of his.

We spent the entire afternoon in Fredericksburg. As promised, one of our stops was to get ice cream. And, oh man, was it good! No, more like amazing. I sampled a few flavors while everyone else gave their orders and by the time it was my turn, I, of course, didn't have it narrowed down. Without missing a beat, Jake ordered the three I couldn't choose between, in the largest cup, and then grabbed us two spoons. Heath made some wisecrack about it, but I was too busy gushing to care.

We ate our ice cream while walking around checking out all the shops on the main strip. We had just stopped, so Alli could go inside one of the shops we had come to, when Jake found a bench and motioned for me to sit with him. I looked up right as Jake scooped another bite of ice cream out of our cup and found myself wondering what was going to happen next year when Jake went to college.

Was he going to want to break up or try to make it work? If we did try, would it work? Long distance can be tough, and I've heard most high school relationships don't make it. I quickly shook the thought out of my head. I didn't want to dwell on something that could interfere with the rest of our weekend.

We stayed in Fredericksburg to eat dinner before heading back to Jake's ranch house. It was about an hour drive, and by the time we got back it was dark outside. We remembered to grab marshmallows while we were in town. So as soon as we got back, the boys built up the campfire and the girls got the s'mores supplies ready to go. We spent our last night at the ranch around the fire and eating more s'mores than I have ever had in my life.

When it got late, we put out the fire and everyone departed to our own rooms. This had been the perfect weekend, and I was in no way ready for it to be over. After spending the weekend falling asleep in Jake's arms, I wasn't sure how I was going to be able to go back and sleep alone in my own bed. We were definitely going to have to make more ranch trips. Because the answer is, I can't. I can't be fine sleeping without being pressed up against him and him being the first thing I see when I wake up.

Once we were back in our room, Jake closed the door and then laced his fingers with mine. "This is going to be a problem for me," he said, looking directly in my eyes.

"What is?" I asked, reaching out and brushing his tousled hair to the side. Though, a part of me was wondering if he was feeling what I was feeling about this being our last night together – our "last night" being the problem he was referring to. At least, I was hoping that's what he was going to say.

"Emma, how I feel about you..." his brows pulled together. Wouldn't you know, that boy even makes frustrated look good? I was trying to focus on what he was trying to say instead of how bad I wished he would lean forward and kiss me, but the look on his face and how his lips were just inches from mine made that very difficult. "Emma, the way you make me feel...I don't ever want to give you up. I don't want to have to take you home tomorrow, and I definitely do not want to not have you wrapped up in my arms when I close my eyes at night." Once he started speaking, the urgency in his words made my heart flutter. All I could think about was needing his lips on mine.

I reached up and circled my arms around his neck and connected my lips to his. There was no hesitation. As soon as Jake felt my lips beg for his to open, he had one hand gripping my lower back and the other tangled in my hair, pressing me into him. He kissed me like he needed me to breathe – like I needed him to breathe. His fingertips gripped into my back, causing a moan to escape my lips and my mind to get lost in that beautifully hazy fog. He trailed kisses along my jaw and down my neck, focusing on that sensitive spot that he discovered drives me crazy. By the time he made it back to my lips, I was completely breathless. I stepped back and lifted my arms, and a smile broke across his lips. I don't know what it's going to be like once we get home, but tonight I'm with Jake and tonight I don't have to worry about that just yet.

Chapter Thirteen

The drive home seemed to go by so much faster than the drive to the ranch house, probably because no one was ready for our weekend getaway to be over. When we got to our cars, we all said goodbye and agreed that we were going to have to make this happen again soon. Jake and I lingered longer than the rest of the group – not able to leave each other just yet.

"Call you later?" he asked, tucking a piece of hair behind my ear.

"Can't wait," I murmured against his lips as he kissed me one last time before shutting the door to my Jeep. He tapped my window three times, causing me to smile as I remembered his words from the night before.

He was laying on his side with his head propped up on one of his arms. "You know, we need a signal," he spoke softly, focusing on the circles he was drawing on my stomach.

"A signal? For what?"

He raised his eyes to meet mine. "For when I want to tell you I love you. When I can't say it out loud, or when we're in a group and I want to be able to tell you what I'm thinking."

I smiled as my body warmed and my heart beat a little faster. "OK...like what?"

He let his free arm drape across the bottom half of my stomach, wrapping his hand around my side. "How about I give you three little squeezes. One for each word." He gently squeezed my side three times. "And if you want to say it back, you can do it four times."

"Four? Why four?" I giggled.

"That way I'll know you're saying 'I love you too'."

"Oh." I bit my lower lip in an attempt to keep myself from grinning like an idiot, but in that moment it was hard not too. It had been a perfect moment.

Like last night, a big goofy grin took over my face as I tapped the other side of my Jeep window four times before driving off.

When I walked into my house, I stopped and talked with my parents before heading up to my room. They asked how my weekend was and what Maya and I did all weekend. I told them we just hung out and ate s'mores. That way it wasn't a total lie because, I mean, we did just hang out and we did eat a lot of s'mores. Regardless, they were none the wiser. They said they were glad I had a good weekend and that they were happy I was home. Then I retreated upstairs.

My sister must have been waiting for me to get home, because as soon as I walked into my room she was not far behind. "Did something happen this weekend?" Kenzie accused.

"No why?" I replied, slightly defensive.

"Yeah...OK." She raised a brow. "Look, I don't know what happened this weekend, but I thought you should know Gabe called the house like a million times looking for you. Lucky for you, every time I saw his number on caller ID I picked up the phone."

Oh crap! Gabe was the one factor I didn't think about in regards to my parents finding out the truth about this weekend. Why didn't I just tell him about this weekend beforehand? It's not like he wasn't going to find out anyway. Then I remembered I never returned his call from Friday. Why did I not think to do that on my way home?

"What? Gabe called the house? Why wouldn't he just call my cell?"

"He said he tried, but you wouldn't answer. I told him you were staying with Maya for the weekend, so he should try getting ahold of her. He said that he did. But when he called her house, her mom said she was staying with us for the weekend."

I didn't have any missed calls other than his initial one. Service must have been bad at the ranch house. God, I hope my parents hadn't tried to get ahold of me too. My eyes went wide.

"Do mom and dad know?" I panicked.

"Also lucky for you, I am great at running recon. So no. And look, I don't know where you two were this weekend, but you should really call Gabe because he seemed concerned."

"Thanks Kenz. I owe you. You're the best!"

"I know, I know. Just add it to my tab," she said with a smile as she walked away, waving her hand in the air dismissively.

I seriously had the coolest little sister. If it weren't for her, I would currently be in deep trouble. I would have to make it up to her. I also needed to call Gabe back. I made another mental note to do that as soon as I unpacked. Although by the time I unpacked my stuff it was time for dinner, and then Jake called, and then I got ready for bed and totally forgot. It wasn't until I heard my window open that I remembered I never called Gabe back.

"Jake?" I called out. I'm not sure why I would assume it was Jake. Jake had only crawled through my window once, and Gabe had done it more times then I could even remember.

"No. Just me. Sorry to disappoint you." I could hear the irritation in his voice as Gabe made his way inside my room, causing me to immediately regret mentioning Jake's name. "Why would you assume I was him anyway? There is only one time to my knowledge that he has even done this. Unless you would like to correct that?" he spit out and then stalked into my bathroom.

"No! He has only done it once!" I don't know why my first reaction was to go on the defense. I mean, Jake is my

208

boyfriend. He has just as much right – no, more right – to crawl through my window if he wants to. "Wait. Why am I defending what Jake does or does not do? That's none of your business anyway," I stomped after him, "And you shouldn't be here."

He stopped and turned to face me. He didn't look angry like I expected him to. He just looked – sad. "Why? Because of him?" If I wouldn't have just heard it in his voice, I would have known just by looking at him. Gabe was a wreck. I could see the hurt all over his face, which made my next words that much harder to say.

"Yes," I choked out. "He doesn't like that you crawl through my window, Gabe," I said in a small voice.

"So what? You get a boyfriend and he gets to dictate when you hang out with your friends? You don't get to make your own decisions any more? Is that it?" The irritation was back in his voice. That, mixed with the fact that he was accusing Jake of being some controlling jerk, did not sit well with me.

"Would you like another guy – one who you knew was in love with your girlfriend – to crawl into her window at night? I don't think so," I snapped. I knew that was harsh, but I couldn't stop the words from coming out. "And I don't like you making it sound like Jake controls me. Because he doesn't. But I know this bothers him; it would bother me. And I love him so..." The look on his face when those words came out was enough to shut me up. It made me want to fix it somehow. But what was there to fix? I can't apologize for loving Jake.

209

"Did you sleep with him?" His words were strained and there was no hiding the devastation in his voice.

"What?" I managed, his question taking me by surprise. Where did that even come from? One minute we were in an argument, and the next Gabe was asking me this and looking worse than I had ever seen him. How could I answer him when I knew the answer to his question would crush him?

"Answer the question, Emma. You were gone all weekend. I know you were with him. Did. You. Sleep with him?" The look on his face alone was enough to break my heart.

"Why does that matter?"

"It just does. Now answer the question."

"Gabe..." My eyes filled with tears. Just because I am not in love with Gabe doesn't mean I want to hurt him. He is one of my best friends, and I hate that his feelings grew stronger than mine. I knew because of that, I was about to ruin the friendship that we had. I never asked for my friend to fall in love with me.

"I know the answer. I can see it all over your face. I just need to hear you say it." There was a harshness in his voice that I had never heard before, and I knew it was because he was hurting.

"Yes," I whispered, unable to look him in the eyes as I spoke.

Gabe choked up. "How long?" I could hear the tears that were threatening, and that made it that much harder to answer him.

"Why are you doing this?"

"How long, Emma? How long have you been sleeping with him?" The hurt in his voice was killing me.

A tear escaped down my face. "This weekend was the first time," I spoke in a small voice with my eyes clamped shut, as if that would somehow make this any better.

"Damn it, Emma, I love you. And I know you love me too," Gabe cried out. "I can feel it when I'm with you, and I can see it on your face."

There was no stopping the tears that were now freely falling. "I do love you, Gabe. Just not how you want me too. I'm not in love with you. But you're my best guy friend, and I don't want to lose you."

He reached out and grabbed both of my shoulders. "Then don't. Choose me instead," he pleaded. "You just said I was your best guy friend. The fact that you had to clarify has to count for something."

How do I explain to him that I only said best guy friend because it was that simple. Maya was my best friend, and he was just my best friend that was a guy – not that, that means he was any less special. "Gabe," my voice trailed off.

"Emma, I've waited over a year for you to see that it was me. I knew I loved you from the moment I first saw you. It was when you and Maya walked onto the courts to practice with us for the first time – the summer before school started. Do you remember that?" I nodded. "You were wearing a white tank top and those short pink shorts that I love, that I couldn't believe you were allowed out of

211

the house in, but I was damn sure glad that you were. You were smiling that big, beautiful smile of yours when you walked up. You didn't look nervous at all, and all I could think about was how I was going to get you onto my court. Because I had to know you. Then, when you looked over at me and shared that smile, I knew I was gone."

"I was terrified," I corrected. Gabe looked at me with a puzzled expression. "I was terrified that day, walking onto the courts with a bunch of high school kids that already knew each other. I was so thankful when you and Dylan asked us to hit on your court. I knew right away that we were going to be friends."

Gabe let out a frustrated sigh. "Maybe I should have made my move earlier. But, Emma, I just kept waiting for you to see that it was me," he growled. "Who was there for you when you were upset over losing your car? Me. Who was there for you when that creep broke your heart? Me. Who was there for you this last year when anything bad happened? Me. I've always been there for you, Em. It's always been me, biding my time and waiting for you to realize..." Gabe's voice cracked, and he looked away as he took a deep breath. "It should have been me." His voice was heavy with grief as he looked up at me. "I've loved you from the beginning. You and your big heart and wide-eyed, bright smile. You took my heart and I can never get it back. You've wrecked me for everyone else, Emma. It's always going to be you. You're it for me."

The pain in his eyes was almost too much to bear. Why did he have to do this? Why did he have to ruin everything? "Gabe..." I let out in a shaky whisper, "I thought we were friends?"

"We were," he said defeated, letting go of my shoulders and dropping his head.

"Wait? What are you saying?"

He looked back up at me. "I can't do this, Emma. I can't watch you love him. It's either him or me."

"Gabe. Don't make me do this!" I cried. "How can you ask me to choose? I love you both, just in different ways." I looked up at the ceiling and took a deep breath, trying to steady my voice. Then I set my gaze back on his. "You're breaking my heart," I whispered.

"Then I guess you can rebuild it with all of my shattered pieces. Because they belong to you. They always will."

That was the last thing Gabe said to me before he walked out of my bathroom and crawled out my bedroom window, leaving me standing there as my brain attempted to realize that I was losing one of my best friends. He was asking me to make an impossible choice. How could he ask me to pick between the boy who had become my best friend and the one that I loved? Numb, I crawled into bed and cried myself to sleep.

* * *

With each new day, I kept waiting for Gabe to come up and apologize; to tell me that we could go back to being friends; that we could go back to the way things were before everything got all screwed up.

But he never did.

I barely even saw him anymore because, apparently, he made avoiding me his new life goal.

I had broken down and cried when I told Maya what happened originally. She had soothed and said everything would work itself out. That day I thought she was right. "You broke his heart, Em," she had said as she stroked my hair, letting me cry. "He just needs time. Give it some time and it will all be all right. You'll see." I remember thinking she was right and that in time we could go back to being friends. To being us. And I let myself be happy under the guise of "time".

Well, the days turned to weeks. Before I knew it, we were getting ready to walk out of school for the last time before Christmas break. I got so used to telling myself not to worry because all Gabe needed was time, and that he would walk back into my life when he was ready, that I didn't realize how long it had been.

That, and I hate to admit it, but Jake is a great distraction. When I'm with him I don't even think about missing my friend. Truth is, when I'm not with Jake, I'm in a group with Jake, Maya, and Evan. The four of us hang out all the time and go on double dates, even though they swear up and down that it's not a date and that they are just friends. So all of that, then throw in studying for finals, and I just didn't realize so much time had gone by since I last spoke to Gabe.

Even though I hadn't spent much time recently with Ryan and Dylan, I still hunted them down before leaving school the last day and told them we needed to do something over the break. They agreed that we should get together, but I couldn't tell if they were being sincere or not. The problem is, Gabe was their friend before they were mine. After Gabe left my house that night, it's like our friends had to choose sides too. Honest to God, this whole thing is like a bad break up. Yet, before I let myself get too worked up about it, I found Jake and wrapped my arms around him, allowing myself to get lost in his embrace.

Jake had gotten good at seeing me and knowing when I was upset over the Gabe thing. He had been genuinely concerned about me when I told him what happened between Gabe and I. Jake had told me if taking the window thing away from him was the issue, he trusted me enough to not let me lose my friend over it. He had even asked if him talking to Gabe would help, but I told him it would just make it worse. So, since then, whenever I needed for him to hold me, he was there with open arms until I was ready to let go. As if he wasn't perfect enough as it is.

Once I trusted myself to be OK, I unwrapped myself from his arms and we met up with Maya and Evan. As the four of us walked out of the building together, Maya was on a roll about all the festivities she had planned for us. She literally had planned out our Christmas break without missing any details. We had movies we had to see, caroling, cookie decorating, Starbucks dates, pizza nights, etc. I kid you not – she even had allotted certain days for Jake and I

215

to go on dates. It was hysterical. A part of me knew her obsessive planning was to keep me busy during the break, so that I would not have time to think about the Gabe thing and I loved her for it. Another part of me wished Gabe could just be my friend again, and that part was still sad.

A few nights into Christmas break was finally a day Maya had planned out as a date night, so she came over to help me get ready for my date with Jake. As usual, when Maya comes over to help me get ready, I made myself comfortable in my bowl chair while she rummaged through my closet to pick out an outfit for me.

I had my legs tucked into my chest as I watched her sort through my sweaters. "You don't have to do this, you know."

"Oh my, sweet little Em. Yes I do! Have you seen what you wear to school? I am not sending you out with Jake without my help," she teased.

"Hey!" I squealed. "I'm not that bad at dressing myself," I laughed. "But you know what I mean. I really would be OK if I had a moment to myself." I looked at my friend sweetly, willing her to see she could still have a life and not worry about me for the foreseeable future.

Maya stepped out of my closet and leaned against the wall, crossing her arms. "Look, bitch. Would you let me wallow in my sadness, withering away all alone if the situation were reversed?" she raised a brow.

"Well not when you put it like that," I laughed.

"So we're good then?" Not that she cared about my answer because she was back in my closet as soon as her

216

words were out. I shook my head as I settled back into my chair. Lord knows I love that girl.

All of two minutes later she was handing me the "Maya approved" outfit and telling me to hurry and change so she could have time to fix me up before Jake got here. When he finally arrived, she walked me to the door and told him it was his turn, kissed my cheek, and then said not to do anything she wouldn't do. I rolled my eyes as Jake walked me to his car.

"Don't you roll your eyes at me, Emma Crawford," she called out.

I turned to Jake. "How does she always know?" I whispered.

Laughing, he wrapped his arm around my shoulder. "I don't know. But tonight you're finally all mine. So how hungry are you, because I'm thinking we should just skip dinner? What do you think?"

I looked over at him and he was giving me big puppy dog eyes, which made me laugh. I swatted his arm before saying, "Uh, no. Dinner first because I'm starving, and then we can do anything you want."

"Anything?" he asked with a sexy smirk, stopping in front of the passenger door and pulling me into him.

I gave him a knowing smile. Thanks to finals, the last two weeks had been all about studying and cramming for tests. Sure we hung out, but we always seemed to end up in a group – leaving us both dying for some alone time. "Yes, anything. As long as you feed me first."

Jake abruptly stepped back and opened my door. "Well get in, woman. We need to go get you food. Are you fine with a drive-through?"

"Jake!" I laughed.

"I'm sorry, Emma," he teased. "Can you blame a guy for trying?" He shot me a wink, closed my door, and then ran around to the other side. Once he was in his truck, he gave me one of his perfect smiles as he reached over and squeezed my hand three times.

"I love you too, you big dork." It made me smile every time he did that. It was our own personal secret – something special that just he and I shared, and I loved it every time.

Jake leaned back in his seat and feigned being relieved as he wiped his hand across his forehead. "Phew. Now what do you want to eat?"

"Mexican?" I looked at him with big pleading eyes.

"Well how can I say no to that? Alright, Blondie, let's go get you some chips and salsa."

* * *

After dinner, Jake laced his fingers through mine as we walked out into the parking lot. His strong grip on my hand and the way that he led me to his truck had my insides knotting up in anticipation. Rather than opening the passenger side door, he gently, but deliberately, backed me up against the side, pinning me in by placing one hand on either side of me as he dropped his head to meet my lips

218

with a soft kiss. "Tell me, Blondie. Now that we've eaten, is the offer of 'anything I want' still on the table?"

The husky tone of his voice made it hard not to claim his lips with mine and take what we both so clearly wanted. He ran his lips across my jaw before letting his lips linger on my neck, causing me to momentarily forget that we were in the middle of a parking lot. Trying to focus on the rise and fall of my chest as I took in slow, deep breaths, I gave my best attempt to regain control of myself before neither of us cared about our current location. Right as I tried to speak, Jake firmly gripped the nape of my neck. "Jake," I whimpered, loosing control of my voice at his touch.

At the sound of my voice, Jake snaked an arm behind my waist, pulling me flush against him as he buried his head in my neck. "God, Emma," he growled. Pulling back just enough to rest his forehead on mine, he leaned us back against the side of his truck. "My parents are going to be gone all night at their friend's Christmas party," he breathed. "Come back to the house with me?" I could hear the question though it sounded more like a demand, causing my stomach to do a little flip.

The urgency in Jake's voice would have had me agreeing to just about anything he said. Yet, I couldn't stop the "what ifs" from playing in the back of mind. "Jake, if your parents got home early..."

"You don't have to worry about that. They usually don't make it home after this party until the next morning. It's one of my dad's college buddies that throws it, and every year they seem to get a little more out of control," he chuckled. "The kids are always invited too. I usually stop by for the food and to say hi to everyone, but this year I had better plans," he said with a sexy smirk. "Besides, you know they wouldn't care if you were still there when they got home. Hell, my mom would probably offer to cook you breakfast."

I knew Jake's parents wouldn't care. The first time I ever went to Jake's house, his mom had set us down and told us to always use protection before going on about her new red lipstick and how this particular shade looked good on everyone. Like it was the most normal conversation in the world. I had been mortified, my eyes going wide and my cheeks turning a deep shade of pink. Mrs. Reynolds had thought I was worried about the lipstick not really being universally complexion friendly. She took one look at my face and then took my hand to reassure me.

"Emma, honey, trust me. It really does look fabulous on everyone, especially with those big blue eyes of yours. You'd be fightin' my son off with a stick. Men never understand the sacredness of a freshly applied coat of lip color."

Jake about fell out of his chair he was laughing so hard before adding, "Momma, I don't think Emma is concerned about the lipstick not matching her complexion."

Mrs. Reynolds looked at me with a dumbfounded expression. "See what I'm talking about. Men never understand the importance of a good lip color."

I was a mixture of in shock and humor about the entire conversation. The only thing I could think to say in return, with a shrug of my shoulders, was, "Men."

Mrs. Reynolds had clapped her hands together in delight, causing her bracelets to clang together, before pushing her chair back from the table. "Alright, I'll leave y'all to it. I know you two don't want to entertain an old lady the entire evening. Emma dear, it was a pleasure visiting with you. Jake will have to get you to come around more often. I miss having the company of another female around this house all the time." She had given us each a hug before leaving to go find Jake's father.

Pushing the memory aside, I took my bottom lip between my teeth as I ran my hands up Jake's chest. "Alright, let's go."

* * *

We pulled into the Reynolds' driveway, and Jake let out a frustrated sigh when we saw a silver Mercedes parked out front.

Leaning his head back, he ran his hand down the front of his face. "Well. Looks like there will be a change of plans. There's no way she'll leave us alone if she's still here. I completely forgot she was getting in today."

"Who?"

"My sister, Quinn. She spent the first two weeks of her break with her boyfriend's family in Dallas, but mom insisted she be here in time for Christmas." Jake looked at

221

me with an apologetic look on his face. "It's about time you met her anyway." His grimace turned into a smile as he reached over and took my hand. "Come on, Blondie. She's going to love you."

Hand in hand we walked through the gigantic front doors of the Reynolds' house. "Quinn? You here?" Jake called out.

"Jake!" Quinn shouted from the other room before making a mad dash to get to her brother. Running up, she threw her arms around him. "Mom said you'd be out all night on a date. I didn't think I'd get to see you until tomorrow." Taking a step back, she turned to me with the same huge smile on her face. "And you must be Emma," she said before hugging me the same way she had Jake. "It is so nice to finally get to formally meet you. The last time I saw you, you were rockin' a cute bikini while a friend of yours invited Jake here to your birthday party. Although, I'm pretty sure she had no idea that I was his sister."

"Yeah, that was my best friend Maya. And it's nice to meet you as well," I smiled. Quinn had the same friendly boldness as her mother. Judging by how excited she was to see the both of us, I had a feeling Jake was right when he said there was going to be a change of plans.

Noticing that she was wearing the same shade of lipstick her mother wears, I took a gamble that she was enthusiastic about her lip color as well. "I love that shade of red. It looks so pretty on you," I offered. You would have thought it was the fourth of July by how her face lit up with my compliment.

She looked from me to Jake, wearing a smile that reached both her ears. "Mom was right. She is a doll!" Looking back at me she took my hand, "Emma, I can tell we are going to be fast friends. Now come with me to the kitchen and we will get a few glasses of eggnog. I want to hear all about the girl who stole my baby brother's heart."

I glanced over at Jake to see that his face was also lit up, and then followed his sister into the kitchen. We talked for about ten minutes before she set her empty glass down and stood up to get a refill.

"You know, Emma. We have a ranch house near Fredericksburg. When the weather gets nicer, we will have to make a weekend out of it. But I don't do this cold weather and can only stay indoors for so long, so I typically avoid the ranch house during the winter months."

"I would love to go back. Before it got too chilly, a group of us went for a long weekend. I love that part of Texas," I lilted.

My words caused her to stop abruptly, and, if at all possible, the smile on her face grew even wider. "You know what, I completely forgot I have somewhere to be. Emma, we will have to get together again before I head back to school. We will grab lunch or something." She quickly rinsed her glass and put it in the sink. "I apologize for running out like this. Jake, I'll see you tomorrow and, Emma, I'll call you about that lunch." She gave us both a quick hug as she spoke, then grabbed her purse, and hurried out to her car.

I looked at Jake for answers as soon as the front door shut. Seeing the question on my face, he scooted his chair closer to mine and placed his hand on my knee. "I'm pretty sure my sister just realized how crazy I am about you."

I was completely confused. "Why is that?"

His hand moved up my leg until he found my hand and then laced our fingers together. "Because I've never taken any of my girlfriends to the ranch house."

"But you said you've taken girls before."

"I've taken friends before, some that have been girls; but it has always been my place to get away with friends."

"I'm sorry...I just. I'm not understanding why it is such a big deal."

Jake chuckled to himself, "And maybe one day I'll tell you. But for now, we have the entire house to ourselves for the rest of the night, and I can think of a much better way to spend our time."

"Is that so?" I teased.

Jake leaned forward and covered my mouth with his. "Mmhmm."

Happy to finally be all alone with Jake, I didn't want to waste any more time sitting at this table and Jake was clearly thinking what I was thinking. So in the next moment, I was standing with my back to Jake. Crossing my arms over my body, I slowly lifted my shirt up and over my head and then tossed it at him. Looking over my shoulder, and as sultry as I could manage, I whispered, "Then what are you waiting for?"

Jakes eyes went wide and glazed over with a hungry look. He scrambled out of his chair and threw me over his shoulder as he walked us toward his bedroom.

"Jake! My shirt!" I squealed.

"Later. I've been waiting all day for this, and I think I've been patient long enough."

The urgency that had been in his voice earlier was back, and it sent a welcome chill throughout my entire body.

Chapter Fourteen

Christmas morning I woke up earlier than I had in years, without an alarm, which was a big deal considering I had been up late talking on the phone with Jake all night. I'm not sure what it was, but something had me up early and full of Christmas cheer. I climbed out of bed and quickly threw a hoodie over my PJs and ran into my sister's room.

I crawled onto her bed and carefully stuck my legs in the covers. Cuddling up right next to her I gave her a light shake, "Merry Christmas, Kenz!"

She let out a groan as she rolled over to see who was shaking her. "Seriously? What time is it?"

"I don't know. A little after eight, I think."

"Then why in the world are you in my room? Has Maya invaded your body or something? You would be so pissed if I disturbed the princess's sleep."

I let out a small laugh. She was right. I'm never a fan of being woken up too early, and eight in the morning after being up late would have resulted in one very grumpy Emma. Yet, I just could not stop the merry mood I was feeling.

"Oh come on, Kenz. It's Christmas! Remember when we were kids, and mom and dad would make us go back to sleep because we would get up at like six because we were so excited?" I put my chin on her shoulder, making a dreamy face about the good ole days.

"Yeah, but we were like both under the age of ten, and how are you so perky? I know for a fact you were still up when I got home last night." She rolled over on her stomach, burying her head in her pillow.

Up when she got home. Wait. What? What was she doing sneaking in so late, and how had I not noticed? "Kenz?" I said slowly, walking my fingers up her back. "Care to share where you were last night that required you to sneak in?" I teased in a singsong voice.

Her body went stiff, and I knew she hadn't meant to say that, which only made me want to know more. "Spill, sister!" I died laughing. "I can't believe little Kenzie has started her teenage rebellion years!"

"Shut it," she groaned. "There are no rebellion years. I just...just lost track of time."

"OK, who is he?" I ran my fingers up her sides, hitting where she was most ticklish.

"He's no one. I mean there's no one," she shrieked.

"Who's he?" I countered in a dreamy tone, as I reached down and pinched her rear, causing her to flip over.

"Uggg. Logan. I was out with Logan. OK?"

She was trying too hard to convince me. I knew it wasn't Logan, but I let it go. Kenzie never was good at keeping secrets from me, and I knew she would eventually spill.

Just then her phone beeped signaling she was getting a text message. Since I was sitting up, I was able to reach across her and snatch her phone before she had time to react. No name – just a number.

We need to talk.

Hold on, I recognize that number. I was rolling the last four digits in my mind, 7424, as Kenz reached over and snatched her phone out of my hands. Ryan. That's Ryan's number!

"Kenz, why is Ryan texting you? And how does he have your number?"

She clamped her eyes shut and puffed, laying her arm across her eyes. "Because I put my number in his phone last night."

"I thought you were with Logan last night?" I pressed.

"What is this, twenty questions? Yes, I was with Logan last night. Yes, we ran into Ryan last night."

"Did you see anyone else?" I was now really curious. I couldn't even get my friends to hang out with me after the whole Gabe thing went down, and now Ryan was texting my sister? After apparently "running" into her last night. He better not be making his move because we aren't on the best terms. Promise to Gabe, or no promise.

"No. He was with some people I didn't know. I only spoke to him briefly, and he was asking about you. He wanted to know how you were doing after everything."

Asking about me? "Oh." Things must be bad between us if he resorted to checking up on me via McKenzie. I watched as she quickly texted something in reply and then turned off her phone.

Then it hit me. "Mom and dad let you go out on Christmas Eve?"

"They let you go out."

"But I was with Jake, my boyfriend. His family does a big Christmas Eve thing. It's not like I went and just hung out with friends."

"Yes, and I was with Logan. My boyfriend. And I went to the church's Christmas Eve caroling thing with him."

"I'm sorry, Kenz. I didn't mean to...look, I just don't know how I got to a place where my closest friends check up on me through my little sister instead of just talking to me. Ya know?"

McKenzie sat up and took my hand. "Hey. It's going to be OK," she smiled, trying to reassure me. "Let's not worry about any drama today, OK? Everything will work itself out. Now, where's all that entirely too early Christmas spirit you had going on all of five minutes ago?"

She was right. Today was Christmas, and I didn't need to let all my life drama effect Christmas morning with my family. I gave myself a mental pep talk and decided to deal with all the other stuff later. "You mean...this Christmas spirit?" I broke out into a Jingle Bells remix, which cued Kenzie to crack up and beg me to stop singing before picking her own Christmas song to start singing.

We must have been singing louder than we thought because eventually we noticed our parents creeping in the doorway holding out one of their phones. It must have dawned on us at about the same time that we were being recorded because almost simultaneously, we turned to face them, placing our hands around the other's shoulders while swaying to the carols we were singing.

After our singing subsided, we spent the morning making cinnamon rolls and eating them while we opened our presents. I was on my third cup of coffee and who knows how many cinnamon rolls later when I finally checked my phone. I had a text from Maya saying, "*Merry Christmas, Em!*" and one from Jake wishing me a Merry Christmas and saying he couldn't wait to see me today to give me my present. I quickly texted them both back and, apparently, was smiling as I sat my phone down. I looked up to see my mom dipping her cinnamon roll in her coffee as she watched me intently.

"Was that Jake you were texting, honey?"

"That obvious, huh?"

230

My mom laughed to herself, "Oh to be young again." She smiled at me sweetly. "When is that boy coming over today?"

"I was actually just about to ask you about that."

* * *

An hour and a half later we had the living room cleaned up, were dressed, and had just started making lunch when the doorbell rang.

"I got it!" I put down the mixer and mixing bowl and ran to the door. Jake was all dressed up in slacks and a red button down shirt. At the sight of him, I threw my arms around his neck while pressing my lips to his.

"Merry Christmas, Jake."

Tightening his arms around my waist he pulled me back in, kissing me once more. "Merry Christmas to you too, Em," he murmured against my lips. He didn't loosen his grip on my waist as he leaned his head back and looked down his nose to meet my gaze. "Now, are you ready to open your present?"

"Yes. But you have to open yours first!" I reached down and took his hand, noticing for the first time the shoebox-size wrapped present in his other. "Come on. It's under the tree." My eyes slowly raised back up to meet Jake's as I wondered what could possibly be in that box.

Jake chuckled. "I see you finally noticed your present. Here, why don't you hold onto this so I can open

231

mine," he offered as we walked inside, taking the short cut toward the tree.

He was acting sort of strange, and I couldn't quite put my finger on why. "O-kay?" Stopping to take the present, I immediately noticed how light it was. *Oh my gosh. It's empty.* I looked up at Jake with a questioning glance, cueing him to let out that cute little chuckle he does. Then, without any sort of explanation, he walked right past me and up to the tree.

"I'm guessing this is mine?" He bent down and picked up the last remaining present under the tree. "You sure you still want me to go first?" He arched an eyebrow as he pretended to tug at the bow.

As curious as I currently was about the seemingly empty box that I held in my hand, I was also really excited for him to open his present. His mom had given me a heads-up about what to get him, and I've been excited ever since. "Yes! Then we will get to this mystery box." I lifted the box up and down a few times while pretending to analyze its contents.

"Whatever you say, Blondie." I could tell Jake was excited as he peeled away the bow and paper, and I bit my lip in anticipation of his reaction. Jake was big on his family's traditions, and even though his mother had given me the idea, I was still nervous for him to open it. He pulled the lid off the box revealing a personalized leather notepad cover, and a smile that seemed to reach both of his ears broke across his face. "Em. This is perfect. How'd you know?"

Apparently all the men in his family were given a personalized notepad cover before going to college. When I had asked Mrs. Reynolds if she had any ideas for what I should give Jake, she insisted this would be the perfect gift. I wasn't sure if I should be the one gifting this family tradition, but she reassured me it was fine and that he would love it. And by reassured me, I mean practically made me promise on the spot that I would get him one.

Seeing his reaction to the gift, all my nerves melted away and pure excitement took over. "I have my ways," I teased. "I also hid a picture of us from the ranch in the back cover, so you'd have something to remember me by."

Nerves were back. I had not thought the last part through. I had been so anxious about whether or not he would like the leather cover, I didn't even think about my decision to put a picture of us in the back. We hadn't even discussed where we would be next year. *What if he wanted to go to college without anything from home holding him back? Why did I not think this through more?* I felt the pink rising in my cheeks as Jake pulled the picture of us out and examined it.

He slid the picture back in its place. Using his free arm, he wrapped it around my shoulders, pulling me into a hug and kissing the side of my head. "This is perfect, Em. I love it," he whispered.

Despite the obvious sincerity in his voice, I was still feeling embarrassed about placing the picture of us in the back cover. "You don't have to keep the picture in there if you don't want to. I just wanted to give you a copy of one of the ones of us from the ranch house," I said sheepishly.

"Everything about this gift is perfect. I'm not changing it in any way." He gave my shoulders one more squeeze before sliding his arm back, with a mischievous look taking over his face. "Now it's your turn to open a present."

I looked down at the present I was still holding in my hands. My mind refocusing on what this featherlight box could contain. I gently tore the paper off, revealing an old shoebox. Glancing over at Jake, I could tell he was loving every minute of this.

"Well go ahead. Open it," he encouraged.

Lifting the lid off the box, I discovered tissue paper, lots and lots of tissue paper. I stuck my hand in the center of it all and found another small wrapped box. Taking another quick glance at Jake, I noticed he looked more excited now than he had a second ago. Returning my gaze to the second wrapped gift, I removed the paper, revealing a little black box. I slowly opened the lid and gasped. Inside was a silver necklace with a white gold heart charm that was lined with diamonds.

"Do you like it?"

My jaw was still dropped as I tore my eyes from the necklace to look up at Jake. "Like it? I love it," I beamed. "Jake, you bought me diamonds. No one has ever given me diamonds before." I took the necklace out of its container. "It's beautiful. Absolutely beautiful."

Jake wore a proud smile as I held it out to him. "Help me put it on?" I raised my hair as he draped the necklace around my neck. "I don't ever think I'm going to take this off. I can't believe you bought me my first diamonds," I gushed.

"And hopefully your last," he muttered under his breath.

"What'd you say?" I asked turning to face him, giving him a quick kiss.

His eyes widened. "Uh. Let's go show your parents." He ran his fingers through all that brown tousled hair, making me wish I could tangle my own hands in it. But no matter how much my parents loved Jake, they probably wouldn't be too crazy about it if they found me making out with my boyfriend in the middle of the living room on Christmas day – or any other day for that matter.

"Great idea!"

I'm sure my face was lit up like a friggin' Christmas tree when I walked into the kitchen. Holding my new necklace out for them to see, my mom and sister both immediately started showering Jake with praise over how good he did.

My dad started laughing while walking over to Jake to slap him on the back. "Well, son. You've done messed up. Buying diamonds for your first Christmas together." His laughter continued as he dropped his head and shook it. "Going to be hard to top that next year."

My cheeks flushed at my father's words. Again, I wasn't even sure if there was going to be a next year.

Goodness gracious, why does that thought have to keep creepin' it's way into my mind? I knew we would have to talk about it eventually, but for now I didn't want to have to keep thinking about the possibility of him wanting a fresh start when he leaves for college. I just want to enjoy the definite time that we have left.

"In all seriousness though, that's a real pretty necklace you picked out, Jake."

Jake was once again wearing a proud grin. "Thank you, sir."

We spent the next several hours finishing making lunch, and then sitting around the table stuffing ourselves with my grandmother's tamale recipe before eating more dessert than my stomach had room for. When we were all too full to move, we slouched back in our chairs. My parents used that opportunity to take turns telling stories about my childhood.

Jake had taken my hand in his and would occasionally chime in with "is that so" or "you don't say" as he would glance over at me and give my hand three little squeezes – prompting me to roll my eyes and feign annoyance before squeezing his hand back four times.

After a long lunch, we all helped clean up before dispersing throughout the house. My parents went to take a nap and Kenzie locked herself away in her room, leaving Jake and I to watch a movie alone in the upstairs media room.

I reclined against Jake before reaching out to hit play on the remote.

Once I sat the remote down, Jake ran his fingers down my arm.

"So what does Maya have on the Christmas break schedule for tomorrow?" he teased.

"Believe it or not, tomorrow is actually a free day. So we can do whatever you want."

"I like the sound of that." The sudden huskiness in his voice caused my breathing to stagger. He nuzzled his head against my neck and began trailing kisses along my collarbone.

"But the day after that..."

"Mmhmm." He sucked at the sensitive spot just below my ear, causing me to take in a sharp breath of air. I could feel him smiling against my skin at my reaction.

"There is a party Maya is dragging me to. It would be a lot more fun if you came with me."

"Well, then count me in."

"That was easy." I turned, causing him to lie flat on his back and letting him pull me on top of him.

"Like you really thought I would say no," he whispered, wearing that perfect smile of his. He ran his fingers through my hair and pulled my head down, connecting his lips to mine.

Chapter Fifteen

I was busily curling my hair, getting ready for the party, while Maya sat on my bathroom counter reading Cosmo magazine.

"I still can't believe he bought you diamonds," she gushed. I secured a roll of hair in my curling iron and looked over at Maya, who had put the magazine down, looking mesmerized as she stared at my neck. "Diamonds, as in plural. I mean look at that thing."

I released the curling iron, taking a glance down at my necklace. Unable to control the smile that tugged at the corners of my mouth, "He did good, didn't he?"

"Pfft. I'll say. What do you do that makes guys keep wanting to buy you nice jewelry?" She playfully swatted me with the magazine. My smile faded into a frown at the reference to Gabe. Seeing the change, Maya let out a breath of air as she reclined against my mirror. "Jeez. I'm sorry, Em. I wasn't thinking."

"S-okay. I'm more mad than sad about it now anyway. How could he just throw our friendship away like that, ya know?" I rolled another piece of hair into the hot iron.

"Come on, Em. I'm not trying to take his side here, but try to think about it from his point of view. In his mind, there was hope for more than friendship." She pursed her lips together and moved them to the side.

"Gah...I know." Setting the curling iron down, I placed both my hands on the counter and looked over at Maya. "I just hate that he had to ruin everything. We were so close, and then he just completely removed himself from my life."

"Do you wish you would have done it differently?" I raised a brow at her question. "Picked Gabe instead?" she clarified.

"No. As much as I miss him, losing Jake would completely break me."

I watched her face shift as she processed what I was saying. "So are y'all going to try to make it work next year then?"

There was that question again, the uncertainty that kept rearing its ugly head. "I don't know," I admitted. "We haven't talked about it, and I'm scared to bring it up in case he doesn't want to have to worry about a girlfriend back home his first year of school." Understanding, Maya nodded her head.

I bit my lip as a smile threatened. "Although, I'm almost positive I heard him utter something when he gave

me my necklace. I'm not one hundred percent certain but..."
I took a breath.

"Yes. Go on."

"Well, I said something about how I couldn't believe he bought me my first diamond. And..." Maya's eyes looked as though they were about to pop right out of her head.

"Bitch! Spit it out! I'm in suspense over here."

"It really sounded like he said that he wanted to be able to give me my last diamond too." I clamped my hand over my mouth and Maya's jaw dropped.

"Shut the hell up!"

* * *

Maya never has liked to get to a party on time. She is a big believer in being fashionably late, something about making a grand entrance or whatever. I've never really been one to care either way, but for her it's crucial so I've always just gone along with it.

I texted Jake once Maya and I were in her car to let him know we were finally on our way and to see if he was at the party yet, but he never responded. Pulling up to the house, I checked my phone once more but still no message. I was trying not to worry about his lack of response, but this was so not like Jake that it was hard not to.

You could hear the music from the street when we got out of the car. Either the whole street was also out of town, or they just didn't care that the neighbor's kids were throwing a party. Once we were both on the sidewalk, Maya turned to me and shrugged, "Maybe he just couldn't hear his phone."

With how loud the music was, that had to be it. Jake had never not texted me back before, and if he was already here there was no way he heard his phone. "Yeah, you're right. It sounds crazy in there."

"Come on. Let's go see if we can find the boys."

Inside, we pushed our way through the swarms of people, making our way to the kitchen. Out of nowhere, a clearly buzzed Evan ran up to us, fighting back laughter. "I'm so sorry, Emma." The lack of control he had over his voice made it apparent that he was a lot more than buzzed, making Maya and I laugh with him. "It's all my fault. Please don't be mad at him."

That got my attention. He was talking about Jake. "Evan, what happened? Is he OK?"

Giggling like a little boy, he draped an arm across Maya's shoulder and put a big wet kiss on her cheek. "Oh, he's more than OK. But, Em, please don't be upset with him. I made him do it. Said it was our last Christmas break together before we all graduate and..."

"There she is. There's my girl," Jake slurred, grinning like an idiot as he stumbled up to us. "She's...so pretty. Isn't she s-so p-pretty?"

Maya and I exchanged glances before I held my arms out to help support my intoxicated boyfriend. "Jake?"

"Hey, Em. I missed you. What took you s-so long to get here?" He snaked his arms around me, dropping his hands to my rear. He stumbled as he took a step forward, attempting to kiss me and almost knocking us over in the process.

"Easy there, cowboy. You are really drunk." I wasn't quite sure what to do in this situation. I've never even seen Jake touch a beer and now he appeared to be having trouble standing on his own.

"Holy shit, Evan." Maya scoffed. "How much has he had to drink?"

Evan swung his head over to look at Maya. Bouncing his finger in her direction, he looked perplexed. "That's a great question."

"P-please don't be mad, baby," Jake slurred, with a concerned expression while clinging on to me.

I attempted to free myself from his grasp before he had a chance to knock us both down. I let out a small laugh as I tried but failed miserably to untangle myself from his arms. "I'm not mad, Jake. I just don't know what to do with you right now. You can barely stand on your own."

Jake let go of me and shot himself straight up. "Nope. See. I'm good," he let out before landing straight on his butt, causing Evan and himself to lose control of their laughter.

I playfully rolled my eyes at Maya before bending over to try to help Jake back up. "Oh yeah. You're clearly fine," I teased.

Hearing the humor in my voice, his smile widened. "It's all that bastard's fault," he pointed at Evan. "I'm s-so happy you're not mad. I was s-so worried you were going to b-break up with me. I haven't even had a drink in at l-least thirty minutes."

Evan almost fell over he began laughing so hard. I sighed as I looked over at Maya and just shook my head. "Come on, Jake. Let's get you off this floor and into a chair. What do you say?" I asked, reaching over to help him up.

"Or you can c-come down here with me." Jake reached up and pulled me down on top of him. He buried his head into my neck as he wrapped his arms tightly around my waist. "You smell good, Em. You always smell so damn good," he whispered slowly.

Even drunk, his words affected me. Feeling his breath on my neck and his arms tight around me almost caused me to forget that we were in the middle of a very crowded room.

"Christ, Emma. Have some damn self-respect. At least get a room before you ride his cock," a familiar voice barked.

Gabe.

Jake instantly tensed at the verbal attack and before I had a chance to respond, he shot back. "Leave her alone, asshole. She ch-chose me, so why don't you just g-get lost?"

I couldn't move. I could barely breathe. Gabe's harsh words had me paralyzed and torn between angry and hurt. He had never been so cruel, especially to me. I didn't even recognize the person speaking to me. Frozen on the ground, I peered into Jake's worried eyes as he grabbed the sides of my face trying to get a read on me.

"So this is who you've become? A little slut that gives it up in the middle of a party?"

Screw being hurt. I was mad. I don't know why Gabe suddenly felt like he could talk to me that way, but it did not go over well – with anyone. I jerked my head in his direction, scowling at him.

At the same time, Jake quickly stumbled to his feet, knocking me off of him. "L-listen, dickhead, I'm warning you. Do. Not. S-speak to her. That way."

Gabe bowed up and let out a cocky laugh, "Or what Jake? You're going to slur me to death?"

Jake stumbled forward as I shot to my feet – concerned one of them was about to throw a punch. At the same time, seeing the growing tension, Evan stepped between them and placed a palm on both of their chests. "Easy there, Jake," he said with a warning glare.

"Yeah, Jake. I wouldn't want you to hurt yourself. Clearly you can no longer handle your alcohol," Gabe baited.

I looked over at Maya who looked as lost as I was. Gabe was goading him, and I wasn't sure why. But whatever this was about, it was working.

Jake fisted his hands at his sides and Evan tensed – ready for whatever was about to happen. "Jake?" he warned once more. "Come on, buddy, he isn't worth it and you are in no shape," he paused and glanced over at me, "to go down this road. Let's just get the girls out of here, yeah?"

Jake turned and looked over at me and seemed to calm down a bit. Facing Evan again, he relaxed his fists. "You're right, Ev. This p-piece of shit isn't worth it."

Evan seemed to relax at his words, leaving me more confused than I already was. I had no idea what was going on. I had never seen Jake so worked up about anything. It was like watching someone I didn't know.

"You know, Jake, I'd leave too if it meant getting some of that sweet ass," Gabe taunted.

His words sent Jake over the edge. Instantly Jake lunged forward, taking a swing and knocking himself off balance. Luckily, Evan caught him so he didn't tumble over.

Gabe let out a satisfied laugh before shooting a wink my direction and taking a swig from the drink in his hand. "Don't look so shocked, Em. I just did you a favor. What are FRIENDS for?" he said maliciously.

I couldn't help myself. Gabe was way out of line. I marched right up to him and slapped him across the face. Instantly, Gabe put his hand where mine had made contact; for a moment his eyes softened, and he appeared to be himself again. Yet, the moment was fleeting. Almost as quickly, his jaw grew tight, a glare replaced the softness, and he stormed off.

Once Gabe was out of sight, Jake took one look at me and then pushed away from Evan and stalked out of the room.

"Jake!" I called out, turning to follow him; but Evan grabbed my wrist and pulled me back.

"Let him go, Emma. He just needs to cool off," he said calmly.

I whipped around to face him. "Cool off? What the heck just happened here Evan? I have never seen him like that. Why do I feel like the only one who doesn't know what is going on?" I could tell my sudden attitude took Evan by surprise.

Evan leaned his head back and pinched his eyes shut before looking back at me. "Look, Em, I know for a fact he never wanted you to see him like that, OK? So just give him some time to cool off."

"Evan, what are you talking about?"

"I know he's told you that he doesn't really drink anymore."

"Yeah. So?"

"So haven't you ever wondered why?"

"No, Evan, I haven't. Why don't you enlighten me?" I snipped.

"Because it's not my place to tell, damn it! But look around, Emma, you're a smart girl. I bet you could piece it together."

I let out a breath in disbelief. *What in the world was wrong with everyone tonight?*

"Fine! If this is how everyone wants to play tonight!" I turned and stormed into the kitchen, Evan and Maya in tow. Grabbing a solo cup off the counter, I grabbed the closest bottle of liquor and poured it in.

"Emma, honey. What are you doing?" Maya asked carefully.

I grabbed another solo cup and shoved it at Maya. "Didn't you get the memo, Maya? Pick your poison and bottoms up."

Before I could think twice about my decision, I tilted my head back and took a huge gulp of my drink. I immediately started choking. Oh my God, that burns! How do people drink this stuff? I sat the cup on the counter, and Maya stepped forward and wrapped me in a hug. As soon as I felt her arms around me, frustrated tears started spilling from my eyes.

"I'm sorry, Em." she whispered. "Tonight has turned out to really suck, hasn't it?"

"Yeah," I sniffed. "What the heck has gotten into Gabe, and why was Evan having to hold Jake back like that?"

"I don't know, Em. None of it makes any sense."

"No. It doesn't. It's like I didn't recognize either one of them."

"Why don't we go find a bathroom and fix ourselves back up?"

"Alright," I nodded, cueing Maya to take a step back. "I'm following you."

Maya took my hand as we navigated through the crowd and found the bathroom. I kept my head down, wanting to avoid the stares from everyone that had just seen our little spectacle. I have never in my life been so publicly humiliated. All I wanted to do was get to a bathroom, take a few deep breaths, collect myself, and then get out of here.

Closing the door behind us, I walked to the counter, leaned over and placed my elbows on the granite, and then put my head in between my hands. I slowly took a few deep breaths before turning and sliding down against the cabinets.

I'm not sure how long I just sat there like that, but when I finally looked up at Maya she handed me a tissue and offered a smile. She made a swiping motion under her eyes, letting me know I had some cleaning up to do. I stood up so I could evaluate the damage. Facing the mirror, I saw I had some serious stray mascara going on. I quickly wiped it out of the way and tossed the tissue in the trash.

Without saying anything, Maya reached inside her purse and grabbed some makeup. She touched up my mascara, eyeliner, and lip gloss and somehow made me look like I hadn't been crying.

After a moment more of silence, Maya took my hand, "Want to get out of here? This party kinda blows." At that, I cracked a smile and we both burst out laughing. It wasn't that funny, but for some reason we couldn't stop.

Once we collected ourselves, I took another deep breath. "Yeah. Let's get out of here. First, I want to apologize to Evan and then this 'piece of ass' is outta here!"

"Hells yeah!" Maya joined in, giving me a high-five!

Chapter Sixteen

Escaping from the bathroom, I made a beeline to the kitchen. My goal was to find Evan, apologize for biting his head off when he was only trying to help, and then get the heck out of here. Instead of finding Evan in the kitchen, I found Gabe, taking shots. Not wanting to deal with any more of his crap tonight, I turned to head right back out before he saw me.

Too late.

"Look who decided to come up for air after getting some," he baited.

I knew he'd had too much to drink and that it was useless to argue with someone in this state. For crying out loud, now he was taking shots! But after what he pulled tonight, I was too mad to care.

"What is your problem, Gabe?" I snipped.

He sauntered over to me and looped an arm around my waist. "I'm not used to you being quite this feisty,

Emma. Is it just for me, or is it Jake that brings it out in you?" He smacked my butt earning whistles from those around us.

"Cut it out, Gabe. You're drunk." Maya said sternly – not hiding her annoyance. Her comment distracted Gabe enough to let me pull out of his grasp.

"Pipe down, Maya. Can't you see my FRIEND and I are trying to have a conversation?"

Maya looked disgusted. "You really are being an ass tonight, Gabe. Emma, will you be OK for like two seconds? I'm going to go find Evan so we can get out of this nightmare." I motioned that I would be fine, and then Maya disappeared into the crowd.

Turning my attention back to Gabe, I took a step backward and then crossed my arms over my chest. "What exactly is the issue here, Gabe? Are you really this upset that I didn't want to date you? Is that what has you acting like such a jerk?"

"Ouch. Low blow, Emmie. And after I did you a favor tonight. Cause isn't that what friends do? Help each other out?" he smirked.

"My God! What are you even talking about, Gabe?" I shouted.

"I thought it was about time you found out about the kind of guy you were really dating. Too bad you decided to give it up to him before you discovered all the skeletons in his closet." My jaw dropped as tears threatened my eyes for the second time tonight. He had just announced to the entire room that I lost my virginity to Jake.

I shook my head in disbelief. Out of all the times Gabe has had too much to drink, I have never seen him act like this. In that moment, I decided that I wasn't going to stand there and try to reason with this version of my friend. If that's even what we were anymore.

I dropped my hands to my sides, signaling my surrender. "Maya is right. You really are being an ass tonight," I let out, unable to hide the hurt in my voice. I turned to go find Maya. I no longer cared about finding Evan. I could apologize to him tomorrow.

"I'm sorry, Em," Gabe said, stopping me in my tracks. Thank God, I finally got through to him. I turned around to find him standing right behind me. He placed his hands on my shoulders as the smirk returned to his face. "I'm sorry I didn't do this sooner." In an instant, Gabe had one hand around my neck and the other gripping the small of my back, pulling me in and firmly planting a kiss on my lips. I struggled to get away, but it was pointless. "I have always used way too much self-control with you – not wanting to ruin what we had. But hot damn if it's not a turn on to hear that pretty little mouth say such naughty words. Tsk, Tsk, Emma."

All of a sudden, a fist went right by my face and hit Gabe square in the jaw, causing him to release his grip on me.

"You're lucky it's me that found you, you dipshit," Evan barked. "Do you have any idea what Jake would have done to you if he had seen you attacking Emma?"

Gabe rubbed his jaw. "And I'm the dipshit? I wasn't attacking Emma. It's called a kiss. Maybe if you ever got some, you would understand the difference."

Evan shoved Gabe into the wall. "You arrogant asshole. Jealousy is a bad look for you Gabe. In case you haven't noticed, Emma kicked your ass to the curb."

Gabe looked from Evan to me before straightening himself up. "You know what, I don't need this tonight. Emma, gimme a call the next time you need a real man to crawl through your window. It shouldn't take you long since his friend here doesn't even know what a simple kiss is."

Gabe turned to leave, heading for the door. The little voice in my head was screaming at me to let him leave – to go find Jake and figure out exactly why Gabe was lucky that he didn't find him just now. But Gabe had crossed a line tonight. First, with the verbal assault and then with whatever that just was. Without even thinking, as soon as he was out the door, I took off after him.

"Emma. Wait," Evan called out.

I stopped and faced Evan. "No. After tonight, I deserve some answers. Starting with Gabe."

"Ah, shit. I need to find Jake," I heard him say to himself as I walked toward the front door.

I spotted Gabe halfway across the lawn and took off in a dead sprint in his direction. "Gabe!"

"Go away, Emma."

"Gabe, stop!"

"Go. Away. Emma!" He yelled.

"Gabe, stop! Stop acting like such a dick." Gabe halted and turned to face me, momentarily looking like my Gabe again, the Gabe I knew before everything got so messed up.

The moment was fleeting because as quickly as he had stopped, he turned back around and kept going, picking up his pace. Although, it had been just long enough for me to catch up to him.

"What do you want, Emma? Can't you see that I'm trying to leave?"

"What do I want? I hardly think that is a fair question after how you've acted all night." I panted, placing my hands on my hips.

"It's all about you, isn't it?" he shouted as he unlocked his car.

Realizing he had no intention of stopping to talk to me, I ran around to the passenger side of his car. Once I had opened the door, I heard my name being called, and I stopped to look back. Jake was sprinting toward me with Evan and Maya not too far behind.

"Emma! Baby, please don't get in that car!" Jake screamed as he ran.

I couldn't stop now. I missed my friend, I was tired of his crap tonight, and I wanted answers. He was going to explain what his problem was if I had to force it out of him.

Hearing the engine roar, I looked down. "Make up your mind, sweetheart. Are you in or out? I really don't give a shit either way, but I'm going to need you to shut the door

253

so I can leave." Clenching my teeth together, I scowled at him as I hopped in and shut the door.

As soon as the door was shut, Gabe peeled out onto the street. I glanced in the mirror to see Jake bend over and brace himself on his legs before turning my attention back to Gabe. "You know, I'm sorry everything didn't work out exactly how you wanted. I'm sorry that you decided you liked me more than a friend and ruined everything! Gabe, what else can I say? I'm just sorry!"

"Are you sorry you fell in love with him? Are you sorry you broke my heart into a million fucking pieces?" he shouted.

"Gabe, stop acting like this! Stop making it seem like I intentionally set out to hurt you. You were one of my best friends, and I hate that you're not a part of my life anymore. Did you know Maya made a schedule to keep me busy all break...just so I couldn't sit around and mope about how much I missed you? I can't apologize for loving Jake. I can't and I won't, but why can't you see that you are important to me too?"

Gabe sped up and gripped the steering wheel so tight his knuckles turned white.

"Do you not see how messed up this is? You just said Maya had to make a schedule so you didn't sit around missing me. Me, Emma! Not him. Why can't you just admit that you love me too, damn it!

I threw my head back into my seat. "I told you. I do love you, Gabe. I love you as a friend, just like I love Maya.

You two feel more like family to me than friends. Why can't that be enough?"

He hit the accelerator as we turned, knocking me against the door. "I told you, Emma. I can't be your friend. I can't sit around and watch you love him. I can't pretend to be OK with just being your friend anymore!"

He continued to accelerate, gaining even more speed, and for the first time I realized how bad of an idea it was to let either of us get into his car with how much he had to drink.

"Gabe, what are you doing? Slow down!" I reached for the seat belt and tried to pull it across my lap, but it got stuck.

"You don't get to make the rules anymore, Em. It's not always about you. Other people have feelings too. I'm taking your ass home, and then you're staying the hell out of my life. Got it?" he shouted.

"Gabe. OK. Whatever you say. Just please slow down!" The seat belt finally went loose and I began to pull it across my body.

"Emma." The pain in his voice, as he said my name, caused me to reflexively look up at him. He was looking right at me with the saddest expression. I couldn't stop myself from reaching over and placing my hand on his cheek.

He nuzzled his head in my hand. "I wish I could just stop loving you," he choked out.

How is it that he could make my heart feel like it was breaking all over again? "Gabe." I let out in a small voice. I turned to face out the window, unable to look him in the eyes any longer. Instantly, my eyes went wide. *Oh my God!* "Gabe!" I shouted as I braced myself for the impact of the crash.

Chapter Seventeen

"Emma! You can't catch me! Try and catch me!" my sister giggled.

I smiled as I watched the two long, blonde pigtails blowing in the wind as McKenzie ran around in the sand in front of the beach house my family had rented that summer. I pretended to jog after her, knowing I would catch her in just a few strides. She may not be that much younger than me, but momma said I had hit a growth spurt and I currently have several inches on her.

"You better run fast, Kenz! I'm right behind you! When I catch you, I get a chance with the rainbow wand!" I teased, causing my sister to erupt in to even more giggles.

Not long after, I caught up to her. Without breaking my stride, I hoisted her up in the air and twirled her around as she squealed in delight. I sat her down, and those big, green eyes were beaming as they looked up at me.

"Again! Again!" she shouted. "But this time give me a head start!"

"OK. One more time, but then I really do want a turn with the rainbow wand."

"I guess you can have a turn now," she said sadly, holding out the wand for me to take.

I smiled at how unselfishly my sister was going to surrender our new beach toy, and for some reason, I just couldn't make myself take it yet. "Nah, you take it for one more spin."

Her green eyes lit up. "Really?"

"Yep. One more good run and then I'll take a turn."

"Thanks, Emma! I'm so happy you're my big sister," she smiled. "I love you, Emma."

"Love you too, Kenz."

"I love you, Emma. I love you, Emma."

Wait. Something's wrong. What's happening? Suddenly, the sky went dark, and I couldn't see McKenzie anymore.

"I love you, Emma."

"I love you too, Kenz! Where are you? Keep talking!" I shouted, panicking that I couldn't see anything.

"I love you, Emma."

"Kenzie!" I cried.

"I love you, Emma. Come back to me!"

All of a sudden, I was in our backyard at home.

"I love you, Emma. Please come back to me!"

"I'm trying, Kenz, but I can't find you, sweetie. Keep talking so sissy can find you." My chest tightened and my entire body filled with pain.

"Please, baby, please come back to me."

Wait. That voice, it doesn't belong to McKenzie. I was in full-blown panic mode. Pain surged through me as I twirled around searching our yard for the owner of the voice.

"I love you, Em. Don't you dare leave me."

"Jake?" The voice. I recognized it. It was Jake's, but where is he? Why can't I see him?

"Come on, Blondie. Come back to me," he pleaded.

"Jake! Jake!" I screamed. *"I'm right here! I'm over here!"* A pounding in my head started, and I thought my legs might give out as the pain throughout my body worsened.

"Please, Emma. I need you. I need you to wake up."

"Jake?" I croaked, as I fought my eyelids open.

"Emma! You're awake!" I registered his voice as a wave of pain surged through me. "You're awake," he said slowly, as my eyelids fully opened.

"Jake?"

"I'm right here, Em. I'm right here."

Once my eyes were fully open, they scanned across the room and I realized I was lying in a hospital bed. "Jake, what happened?"

"What's the last thing you remember, Em?" he asked carefully.

"Um. I um. I was getting in a car. I was getting in Gabe's car. Oh my God! Where's Gabe?"

Jake's jaw tightened, and I could tell he was trying to stay calm. "Relax, Em. Gabe is fine."

"Then why do you look so upset?"

"Emma, baby. Let me go get your parents. They went to grab a coffee."

"Jake. Tell me what happened."

Jake's hand tightened around mine, causing me to realize for the first time that he had been holding my hand this whole time.

"Jake?"

"You were in a car accident, Emma. You weren't wearing a seat belt and you hit your head really hard."

I reached up with my other hand.

"Drop your hand, Em. You have a lot of stiches."

I sighed as I dropped my hand back to my side. "Well, that explains the splitting pain in my head, I guess."

Jake let out a small laugh, "Yeah, I guess it does."

"Gabe was driving, wasn't he?"

Jake tensed up again at the mention of Gabe. "Yes. He was," he swallowed.

"Well if I'm here, where is he?" I pressed.

"Not here," he said flatly.

"Jake. What are you not telling me?" Concern grew as the memories from that night flooded in.

"Emma, he should have never let you get in that car. He was in no shape to drive even himself."

"Jake?" I questioned slowly.

He took a deep breath. "Emma, when you got in his car, I panicked. I knew he had been drinking. Then, when

Maya told me he had been taking shots, I almost lost my mind with worry. I told Maya she had to drive since she was the only one that hadn't had anything to drink, and Evan and I hopped in her car. When we found you, y'all had already crashed." Jake looked away, but I could still see the tears building in his eyes.

"I'm so sorry, Jake," I don't know what possessed me to get in that car. I knew he had been drinking, but for some reason that red flag just didn't go off like it should have.

Jake looked back down at me, and a tear fell down his cheek. "When we got here, they wouldn't let me see you. They said that you were lucky to be alive, and that they were stitching you up and making sure everything else was OK. The doctor eventually came out and told us that you were stable, but they still wouldn't let me see you because I wasn't family."

"But you're here now. How?"

He smiled. "Your parents took one look at me and – when they saw the state I was in – insisted that they let me back to see you. I just can't tell you how happy I am that you're awake." He bent down and placed a kiss on my hand. "Baby, I'll be right back. I have to go get your parents. They have been worried sick." He stood up, gently placed a kiss on the side of my head, and walked over to the door.

"You still haven't told me what happened to Gabe." I let out, causing him to briefly pause before continuing out the door and shutting it behind him.

All of the worry over the possibilities of what could have happened to my friend was pushed aside as my parents walked in with my sister directly behind them. Each one looking like they have been up all night.

My mom rushed to my side as soon as she saw that my eyes were open. "Emma, I am – we are – so happy that you are awake. We have all been so worried," she soothed. "Can I get you anything? Do you need anything? Are you in pain?"

I forced a smile. "I'm OK, mom. I mean – I'm as good as I can be."

"Of course you are, honey. Just let us know if anything changes, and we will have a nurse in here right away. OK?" she smiled sweetly.

"OK. Thanks, mom."

I looked over at my dad, who still hadn't said anything, and almost broke out in tears because of the concerned expression on his face. "Hey, dad."

"Hey, my beautiful little girl," he choked out as he walked closer to the side of my bed and took one of my hands.

His reference to me being his little girl made me let out a small laugh. "Dad, I'm not so little anymore and I haven't looked in a mirror yet, but I'm pretty sure it's safe to say that I don't look beautiful in my current state."

He gave me a warm smile. "You couldn't not look beautiful if you tried, and you will always be my little girl."

"Oldest little girl," McKenzie added with forced sarcasm, trying not to sound as worried as she so clearly was.

I couldn't help but smile at my sister's attempt to put on a brave front. "Hey, Kenz. You've been uncharacteristically quiet over there," I teased, which earned me a genuine smile from her.

"Yeah, well, I didn't want to interrupt the Emma Show," she attempted to joke, which made me laugh harder than I expected, causing me to wince as I was reminded of the pain.

"Sorry, Em," she said, the grief returning to her face.

"Kenz, get over here. I'm fine."

"Clearly," she said in disbelief as she made her way to my side.

"Seriously, I'm OK. I'm not dead." As soon as the words came out, all the worry about Gabe came flooding back into my brain. Along with the question of, why hasn't anyone told me about him yet?

"But, Em, you could have been," my sister's voice broke, causing my mom to retreat into my dad's arms. "Don't ever scare me like that again, OK? I still need my big sister," she whispered.

I reached over and took her hand as my eyes filled with tears at her words. "Kenz, I'm not going anywhere. I'm afraid you're stuck with me. OK?"

She forced a smile as she nodded her head to agree with me, while wiping a tear from her eyes.

263

After giving everyone a second to collect themselves, I took a deep breath and then addressed the one piece of information no one had volunteered. "Where is Gabe?" I asked to no one in particular. For a brief moment, you could have heard a pin drop in the room.

"He's fine, honey. He was released last night with a cast on his arm and a few bumps and bruises," my mom finally spoke up with a tight-lipped smile, causing me to immediately release the breath that I didn't even realize I was holding.

"Yeah, and a broken face," McKenzie let out under her breath.

"Wait? What?" I looked at my sister.

"You should have seen it, Em," she said as her eyes went wide. "It took both Evan and Dylan to pull Jake off of him. It was crazy! Jake took one look at Gabe when he walked out into the waiting room and then all of a sudden Gabe was on the floor and Jake..."

"McKenzie," my mom cut in sharply. "That's enough."

This was a lot of information to try to process all at once. "So if Gabe's OK, why has everyone avoided just telling me what happened instead of letting me assume the worst?"

"He's just not everyone's favorite person right now, sweetie. He should have never let you get in his car – much less allowed himself to get behind the wheel," my mom said as kindly as she could manage.

"No, he shouldn't have," my dad added, not bothering to hide the anger in his voice. "I'm just glad Jake got ahold of him before I had the chance to..."

"William!" my mother cut in again.

There was a knock on the door followed quickly by Jake poking his head back in.

"I wanted to give you guys a moment, but is it alright if I come back in?" He was clearly asking just to be polite because by the time he was finished with his question, he was already sitting in the chair by my bed and taking one of my hands in both of his.

"Jake, you know it would have been alright if you needed to go home and get some rest or at least take a shower," my mom said, wearing the most genuine smile she had since she first saw that I was awake. She let out a warm laugh before continuing, "Come on you two. Let's give these guys a minute." She gave me a little wink before shooing my dad and sister out of the room. She stopped briefly to put her hand on Jake's shoulder and gave it a light squeeze before exiting behind the rest of my family.

Once the door was closed, I looked back over at Jake. "You've been here all night?"

"Emma, I was so worried about you. There is no way I was about to leave you. They would have had to drag me out."

"You've been here all night," I repeated as a small smile broke onto my face. My eyes glossing over, again, as I let those words sink in.

Realizing I was making more of a statement than re-asking my question, Jake leaned closer to me and let one hand brush the side of my face. "There is nowhere else I'd rather be."

I smiled while giving his hand a squeeze before thinking about how that might hurt if his hands were sore. Given what Kenz had said, I quickly released my grip. "So I guess I should ask how you're doing, or how your hands are doing at least?"

Jake clamped his eyes shut, as soon as my words were out, and sucked in a breath. He lowered his head, and his demeanor quickly changed from happy and relieved to worried and anxious. "Before they told us you were OK, he came out in the waiting room. Just walked out, wearing only a cast on his arm. Emma, I was so upset. He is the reason you are here right now, and he walked out in only a cast."

After a few seconds, when he still didn't raise his head back up, I squeezed his hand three times. Glancing back up at me, his eyes were full of worry. "I'm so sorry. I was just so mad I couldn't see straight and he..."

"Did it make you feel better?"

He cringed, "Yeah. It kind of did."

I gave a little shrug, "OK then."

"That's it? I'm off the hook?"

A small laugh escaped my lips. "Yeah. I guess so, and from what I hear he's lucky it was you and not my father. Plus, and this might make me a terrible person, but I sort of feel like he deserved it. Don't get me wrong. I'm glad that he's OK. It's just, after everything that's happened...I guess what I'm trying to say is, I understand why you did it."

I watched as a look of relief washed over his face as everything I was saying sunk in. "Thank God," he let out, sounding more like himself once he realized I wasn't upset with him. "I was so worried that once you found out what happened with Gabe...and top that off with what happened last night," he paused to let out a nervous breath. "Listen, I know Evan said something to you about my past."

"About that. Jake..."

"Look, Emma. There's a reason I don't drink much anymore. I don't like who I can become once I've had too many. And I've been in a lot of fights because of it."

"You normally win those fights, don't you?" His eyes grew wide and worry returned to his face. "It's just how Evan reacted last night toward Gabe. It didn't seem like you getting hurt was ever really a problem."

He nodded his head in understanding. "No, Emma. Me getting hurt was never usually part of the problem."

"Well, is that who you are anymore?"

"No. It hasn't been who I am for a while now."

"Then what's done is done. You can't change your past, and you can't worry about it either. I don't even know that guy you say existed. I do know the guy in front of me, and that guy I'm crazy about."

A smile broke across his face as he chuckled that chuckle of his that I love so much. "I'm pretty crazy about

267

you too, Em. I don't know what I'm going to do without you next year."

And just like that, there it was. The dreaded next year. "Jake, about next year." My eyes shut as tears threatened. Blame it on the pain and the emotional toll from everything that has happened.

"Hey. What is this? What about next year?" Concern was evident in his voice.

I popped my eyes open as I looked over at him. "What are we going to do next year?"

"Well, not being able to see you every day is really going to suck, but it's only for a year. Then you will be at A&M with me. And then I'll be able to see you every day if I want to," he said simply. "Better yet, several times a day if I want to," he finished with a sexy smirk, which caused me to laugh out loud, resulting in a wince as I was reminded of the pain my entire body felt. "Sorry. I won't make you laugh anymore. I wasn't even thinking."

Once the pain went down, I looked back over at Jake, "So you want to stay together next year?"

I barely got the words out before he responded. "Hell yeah! Don't you?" His reaction caused me to laugh out loud again, resulting in another wince. "Sorry again," he grimaced. "I wasn't expecting you to say something so crazy."

"It's just...long distance is hard, and they say that most high school relationships don't make it."

"Who are they? They clearly aren't us. Besides, there is always the exception to the rule."

"Well, yeah but..."

"No buts." He stood up out of his chair and carefully sat down next to me on the bed. "Emma, do you love me?"

"Yes."

Smiling his perfect smile, he gently leaned down and placed a soft kiss on my lips. "Then if I have to drive back every weekend that first year, I will." He let out a small laugh as he shook his head. "Emma Crawford, I love you so much, and you're crazy if you think I'm going to let you get away that easy. I don't care if any other high school relationship in the history of the world has ever made it. All I care about is that we will. You're my whole world, Emma, and there is no story or version of my life without you in it." He paused for a moment and looked at me with a smile that reached both of his ears. "Em, you and me, this is how it ends. Us together...happily ever after...however you want to say it," he continued, pausing again to reach up and wipe the tear that had escaped down my face with his thumb. "We're the exception. This," he said gesturing between the two of us, "is the exception."

There was no stopping the tears that were now free falling down my face. I didn't even know it was possible for my heart to feel as full as it did in that moment.

I reached up, needing him to feel everything that I was feeling, and took the sides of his face in my hands – slowly bringing his lips to mine and stopping right before they connected. "Point Jake," I whispered against his lips before kissing him with everything that I had.

Epilogue

Jake

"Jake. Listen man. You need to get your shit together."

I stuck my hands in my suit pockets while I looked over at Gabe, as he bent down to plug the lights into the outlet on the back porch. He was right. I was so nervous I could barely keep my hands from shaking. I just knew I was going to take one look at her when she got to the ranch house and mess it all up.

Every minute that went by seemed to go by slower and slower. All I wanted was my girl here and for her to say yes as I slipped the two and a half carat, princess cut diamond on her finger. If that didn't happen soon, I'm pretty sure I was going to sweat straight through my suit or suffocate due to the lack of air that didn't seem to be getting to my lungs.

270

The lights lit up and Gabe and I exchanged glances, both smiling at each other at the sight. They were perfect; Emma was going to love them. So now, the lights were up, the flowers were set, and the tables were in place. All that was left to do was to light the candles that lined the back porch and that were on each table. As nervous as I was, I couldn't wait to see her face as I got down on one knee and asked her to marry me.

Quinn had Dylan, Ryan, and her husband helping her in the kitchen as she slaved away making food, sides, and desserts all afternoon. While Gabe, Evan, and I took care of getting everything set up outside.

I just couldn't believe it was finally happening. Our parents and other guests had arrived not too long ago and were getting ready in their rooms. Knowing Emma, I knew she would want those she cared the most about to be able to share in the celebration of our engagement. I had set everything up so that after I proposed our family and closest friends could be here to celebrate with us. The only people missing were the girls.

Emma was under the guise that they were having a girls weekend, one last hurrah before the start of her senior year at Texas A&M. She even thought I was out of town for work. About a week ago, Quinn had invited her and the girls to the ranch house for the weekend. Before that, Maya had been in charge of keeping this weekend wide open. So in the not too distant future, Emma would be arriving with Maya, McKenzie, and Jade – who had been a part of the group since the girls' freshman year.

271

"Everything is all set around the corner for ya man," Evan said as he walked back over to Gabe and I. "Want to come take a look at it?"

I glanced down at my watch. "Sure thing, but we need to hurry so I can go inside and cool down before she gets here. Is it unusually warm out here to either of you two?"

Gabe and Evan exchanged glances before bursting out laughing.

"Yeah, well, we'll see how you two feel before you propose to the love of your life."

They looked at each other once more before once again cracking up.

"Everything is going to work out how it's supposed to. This place looks great. Thanks to Quinn and her slave-driving ways, the inside looks perfect and the food looks and smells incredible. Emma is going to be in girl heaven when she gets here. Plus, it helps that she's crazy about you – has been ever since she met you. Though for the life of me, I can't figure out why." A sly smile broke across Gabe's face before he shot me a wink. "Even without all this," he gestured to all the immaculate decorations, "she would say yes. So chill the hell out," he laughed.

There was a time when I would have told you that you were crazy if you had said that Gabe would grow to become one of my closest friends – friends at all for that matter. After the accident, we couldn't even be anywhere near the other. But looking at us now you would never guess that. I suppose we have Jade to thank for that, and I

272

wouldn't be surprised if Gabe and Jade weren't too far from this themselves.

It's funny how things work out. Who would have known that Ryan would have beaten us all to the altar? Eloping of all things. Not everyone was particularly thrilled that they did that, but I have a feeling the news they are going to share tonight will be received well by everyone. Ryan had pulled me aside earlier to ask if I minded if they broke the news tonight. I assured him it would only add to Emma's excitement before congratulating him myself.

"Alright, man." Evan slapped me on the back, breaking my train of thought. "Maya just texted saying they were ten minutes out. Let's get these candles lit and you in your place."

ACKNOWLEDGEMENTS

To my readers. Thank you so much for taking the time to read Emma and Jake's story. It means the world to me.

To my amazing, patient, and handsome husband Chris. Thank you from the bottom of my heart. I have lost count of the amount of times you listened to me brainstorm, read the same section over and over again while I tried to explain what I was thinking, and just my general babble about this book. Not to mention the hours of your life you selflessly gave up to help me piece through this story and relearn grammar rules (including the ones we never knew existed). I'm pretty sure you know more about comma usage at this point than I do. I am a lucky girl to have a number one fan, unofficial editor, and best friend wrapped up in one sexy package! Thank you for helping me chase my dream. I love you.

Aleah Esparza – Where do I begin? This book would have never happened if you wouldn't have demanded to know more. Thank you for reading and then re-reading sections of this book and for listening to my many thoughts and ramblings. You will never know how much I truly appreciate your enthusiasm for this story and for falling in love with the characters as much as I did.

Alison Cote and Sherri Sedlacek – To my original book groupies. The excited energy you two ladies had about this book was infectious. Thank you for reading along with me and cheering me on. Thank you for talking about the characters like you knew them, and for taking such a genuine interest in this project. Last but not least, thank you for sneaking my book into places because you couldn't put it down!

Jana Mietchen – There are no words to express how truly grateful I am for you. Without you this book would have remained basically unedited. Thank you so much for helping me make my story the best it could be! I am beyond lucky to have had you.

About The Author

Brittany Wynne was born in Odessa, TX. She attended Texas A&M University where she graduated with a degree in education. She now lives in The Woodlands, TX with her husband Chris and their fur-baby, a maltipoo, named Hank.

A self proclaimed book addict, she contributes her love for reading as to why she developed the writing bug. When she's not brainstorming new character and story ideas, she can be found reading, shopping, spending far too much time on instagram, and binge watching her favorite shows with her husband and pup.

Made in the USA
San Bernardino, CA
15 July 2016